'Worlds Within Worlds tackles the problem of identity in the age of technological anonymity. Ella Smith is an independent author and editor whose online life crashes into reality with disturbing implications. The book questions how much of one's true self can—and should—be broadcast to the world.' Amy Spahn, literary critic.

'This is riveting stuff, part magical realism dreamscape, part taut psychological thriller, and I was literally on the edge of my seat when the final twist – and what a twist it is – came around. Phew, what a ride! I can honestly say this is the best book I have read this year. ' Frank Kusy, author of Rupee Millionaire.

'One of the most innovative and original works I have read in a long time. The book is compulsive enough to collapse time. ' Richard Bunning Reviews

'Contemplative story about the creative process that's also, amazingly, a page-turner. I put everything else aside and read it in a single afternoon.' Amazon Vine reviewer Dream Beast.

Worlds Within Worlds

Tahlia Newland

Foreword

What follows is fiction. Prunella Smith is an editor and an author like me, but she is not me. Though we were both dancers and are both Buddhist practitioners, she is not me. In all those areas, she took the paths I didn't take, and her opinions do not necessarily reflect mine. The only way our lives are alike, apart from the author/editor connection, is that she lives in the bush in Australia, owns a cream Burmese cat and is given to metaphysical musings.

Although I have spoken to authors who have experienced intensive cyber bullying and been the recipient of some of the milder forms of attack myself, the events and characters in this story—apart from Merlin—are not based on any real event or person. Any resemblance is purely accidental.

This book has several psychologically interconnecting threads—the structure is somewhat like a multi-layered strand of DNA—and they use different tenses. This is intentional, so is the repetition of certain sentences and the poor grammar and punctuation in Dita's communications.

Thanks to Annie Mitchell, Brian Sfinas, Pete Morin and Charles Ray for their contributions to Dita's bullying verbiage, and to Alexes Radovich, Amy Spahn and Rose Newland for their beta reading. Your input really helped.

I hope you enjoy my small offering to contemporary metaphysical literature.

1

Ordinary Reality

Ordinary reality peels away, as if some cosmic hand wipes a film from my eyes. The sounds of cicadas, frogs, crickets and trickling water take on a vibrancy that thrums through my being like a mantra. Ripples from the gentle waterfall spread across the pond, like the vibrations of my mind spreading to all humanity and beyond. Never have I seen trees so luminous with life or such a depth of blue in the pristine sky. The forest and the sky have not changed, merely my perception of them. The limitations of my mind have fallen away and I glimpse beneath the veil.

This is where I belong. This is where I aim to be in every moment of my day. Let the storms of life rage around me. In this, I will remain firm. This is not a thought. It is a knowing.

Movement.

Like a fish rising from the depths of a clear, still pond, some remnant of ordinary mind surfaces. A desire. Work calls. Someone must put food on the table.

I sigh. And the veil falls back as I turn my mind to the mundane. As a self-employed editor, I make my own work hours, but I don't always take the time I should for the things I should. Like housework. Argh. Why bother when in a few days everything is dirty again?

I'd love a Brownie. Not the chocolate eating kind—though I'd like that too. No. The Brownie I'd like is the Fae kind—the kind that does your house-work while you sleep—but it's dangerous to commune with the Fae world. I don't believe in faeries anyway. Peter Pan's Tinkerbell would die if it were up to me.

I laugh at the distraction and the thought-stream fades.

I should be working on the editing job I scored a full edit on. If I don't make the deadline, the agree-ment says the author can ask for her advance back. And I've already spent the money on the overdue rates bill. The rest of the job will pay the credit card off nicely. Without it … I wonder briefly if I could go back to stripping to supplement my meagre income. *Not without learning martial arts first.*

I turn back to my computer.

The story of Kelee's World punctuates my daily life of silence and solitude up here in the bush. She lives in an ancient village with horses and cobblestones instead of wallabies and rainforest. And demons, not wombats, lurk beneath her house. Hers is a fictional world, yet it has a reality all of its own, and for her, it's far more real than mine.

2

Kelee's World

Kelee slammed the dusty tome on the table and froze. The thump had sounded far too loud in the silent household. But no querying mother's voice rang along the corridors, and Kelee reminded herself that the walls were thick stone. She breathed again. Dust motes danced in the sliver of rising sun that pierced the library's gloom. She shouldn't have to wake before everyone else just to read a book, but that was the way in Menhir Village when the topic was ancient Warrior lore.

Horses' hooves clattered on the cobblestones. Kelee raced to the window. Who else was up at dawn? She peered through a lead-rimmed pane in time to see a black-haired man mounted on a regal-looking horse canter from the compound, his deep purple cloak streaming out behind him. Kestril. Her brother. Where was he going and why? He often disappeared for the day, but no one bothered him about it. Mother, however, would make a fuss if she didn't know where her precious daughter was at every moment.

Kelee looked down at her slim-legged trousers and black knee-high boots. Magan men wore the same style, along with the same kind of soft cotton shirt and leather waistcoat. Only the wide leather belt dotted with pockets and the black hair tumbling past her shoulders marked her as a modern woman. Mind you, few men would choose cerise as the colour of their trousers, and lavender for their shirt.

Kelee's sword still rested on the table by her bed to reassure her mother, should she enter the bed-chamber, that her daughter was not far away. Magan women gained the same education as men—those of noble blood at least, and others if they could afford it—but when it came to personal freedom, only daughters ever showed the results of sexual indiscretion. It mattered not for the common folk, but chiefs' daughters were 'encouraged' to marry according to their parents' wishes, and in Magan society a pregnancy made you married to the child's father with or without a ceremony.

Kelee smiled at her secret—Miramar's herbs. Magic couldn't prevent procreation, but the right kind of herbs could; the herbs of a skilled healer like darling, silver-haired Miramar with the smiling eyes. She'd taken them long before she and Slade took their passion beyond the furtive kisses that had fired her desire.

Her gaze wandered across the courtyard to the grey stone walls and slate roof of the stables. Kestril had closed the double wooden doors behind him, but Slade would arrive to open them soon. Perhaps an early morning ride was in order. A note to mother should suffice, so long as they weren't gone too long. The twinkle in her brother's eye told her that he suspected her friendship with the groom was more than it seemed—little escaped Kestril's notice—but she could trust him not to speak of it; he had too many secrets of his own.

With a sigh, Kelee turned from the window and returned to the book. Miramar had told her she would find it somewhere in the recesses of the library. This book, her mentor had explained, was a doorway to the old Magan ways to power—a power that came not from the sword or the wand, but from the mind. You can lose a sword or a wand, she had said, but your mind is always with you. Once developed, no one can take your inner power away from you.

You can still lose your mind though, Kelee thought with a giggle.

3

Dita

Hmmm. I nod my head, satisfied with the results of my edit, but I'm a little worried. This job could take longer than I thought. I scan the next few pages. Yep, same faults. It looks good on the surface, but the author often says the same thing in a couple of different ways. Combining sentences and paragraphs into one to make it more succinct and better paced makes for time-consuming editing, but that's what's needed. Damn. I should have asked for more money.

I edit a few more pages, then, needing a break from the concentration, I open my browser.

An author I just posted a review for has sent me an email. My mouth slackens as I read it, and a prickly heat works its way up my spine and over my face. Sally, my publisher's marketing manager, warned me this could happen, but I never thought it would—not to me.

Ella, (not even a 'dear')
When I offered you the opportunity to appraise my book and post your review, I had no idea what a vindictive, jealous

8

My eyes widen I can't believe the vehemence behind the words. *Legal action?* Anxiety pools in my stomach. *Little care or integrity?* Anger wells up. How dare he? After all the time I put in to ensure the review was as polite and as constructive as possible. But it's the word *unethical* that really stings. Me, unethical! The review's honesty is a testament to my ethics.

And he can't even spell disrespectfully!

How dare he complain after practically begging me to read his book? And after, through some misguided sense of responsibility to him, I kept wading through his overwritten and cumbersome prose long after I wanted to stop. I should have told him to give readers a break and never write another word; instead I struggled to find something positive to say about it. I did all that for him, and he abuses me!

And … I'd made it clear the review would be honest. He'd agreed to that. And now this. Did he think I was kidding?

My mind swirls with indignation, and the unfairness of it all adds righteousness to my anger—a nasty brew, but seductively intoxicating. Sure, sometimes it hurts to learn the truth, but he should have had a professional check it out BEFORE he published. Perhaps Dita launched his terrible book with such fanfare that he believed his own hyperbole. The cover is actually excellent—he should have stuck with graphic design—but it lures the unwary buyer, like the stunning flowers of a carnivorous plant. It looks good, it must be good, right? Wrong. That's why I had to tell his prospective readers the truth.

I suddenly realise that my teeth are clenched and my body tense. Anger has muddied my clarity, and calm has fled in its wake. I've fallen prey to my emotions as surely as Dita had when he wrote that email.

I take a deep breath and exhale slowly, letting my frustration sink to the bottom of my mind like mud in a pond. I'd like to be able to dissolve it completely, but that might be asking for a bit much right now.

Should I take the review down?

No way. My response is swift and determined. I will not be bullied into something—anything. And taking it down would leave the reading public with no indication of how terrible the book is. That wouldn't be fair on them. How can I leave nothing to counteract all those fake five star reviews? *They have to be fake, don't they?* Surely, no one could honestly think that book warrants five stars?

I shake my head and remind myself not to get distracted.

The threat of legal action, though initially disconcerting, rings hollow, so I don't concern myself with that. I figure I should simply delete the offending mail and forget about it, but the desire to defend myself is strong. My ego wants to retaliate, but that isn't the Buddhist way—it isn't the smart way either. I'm not going to fall into that trap, but I do think I need to respond in some way. Something that will smooth his bruised ego.

I spend far too long agonising over what to say and finally email a bland but hopefully non-inflammatory reply:

Dear Dita

I'm sorry that you found my review hurtful. It was not my intention. My aim in writing reviews is to be of service to both readers and authors, and to achieve any real benefit to either, I must be totally honest. I assure you that I consider my words carefully and try to be as objective as possible.

Once again, my apologies for any hurt that I have inadvertently caused you.

Prunella Smith.

Then I realise how much time this guy has cost me. Precious editing time wasted on something that should never have happened! I have a job to finish and not nearly enough time to do it in.

'I've bought adverts for the release day,' the author of Kelee's story had written in her email, 'so if I don't get the book out in time, I will have wasted that money, and I will ask you to return the advance.'

I have to consciously release the tension in my jaw. I will not let this get under my skin.

It's over now. Finished. I can forget about it.

I stand, jump up and down a few times, and shake my limbs to shake the amateur author out of my head. I'm about to sit down again and go back to work when I realise that he's still there, lurking in the background, just waiting to stir up my anger and pounce on me when I least expect it. If I don't get rid of him, he'll turn the veil into a steel door, and I want to be on the other side. With my head in the right space, I can work fast. With a saboteur in there ... I head towards the back door. I can't do anything about the attack, but I can do something about the concentration.

A stitch in time, my grandmother used to say, saves nine.

4

The Yogi

Merlin, my cream Burmese cat, trots at my heels and yowls. I grab a sash from the back of the couch in the studio and wiggle it along the floor. He scoots after it and pounces. His claws dig in and hold tight when I try to pull it away.

'Ah, Merlin.' I sigh. 'What do you think I should do when an author abuses me?'

Send him a furball disguised as a chocolate. I speak for him—in my mind. If he really could talk to me, I'm pretty sure that's what he'd say.

I scoop him up and carry him—purring all the way—to my meditation room. He doesn't wriggle as we walk through the garden, just looks around wide-eyed. Little birds abound in my leafy garden in the rainforest, and Merlin loves watching them flitter from one shrub to another.

I'm relieved to leave the cyber-world behind. It's unreal compared to the three dimensional world around me, and yet it can take on a frightening reality. Like Kelee's world, the cyber-world is merely black symbols on a white background, but human minds flesh out the symbolism and make it real.

I need to get out of my head.

I open the rickety door into the old one-roomed cabin and plonk Merlin on the floor. He's off in an instant, sniffing for mice, and I have to growl at him when he looks like he's about to jump on my shrine. He shoots me a look that says: *Okay. Fine. What-ever!*

I light the candle and sit on my low meditation chair.

Tension falls off me immediately. The meditation posture and the sacred silence in a room imbued with the remnants of countless hours of meditation automatically relaxes me. The expression 'rolling off in waves' comes to mind. My gaze softens and I smile; the problems of the cyber-world fade from my mind. Dita may think he's causing me pain, but he's the one who lives in a mind filled with hate.

My meditation teacher stares back at me from his photo in the centre of the wooden shrine. Photos of his own teachers flank him. They're like my spiritual grandfathers and grandmothers. On each end of the top shelf sits a gold and brass statue, Guru Rinpoche—the master of all the Tibetan masters—on one end, and White Tara—the goddess of compassion—on the other.

Images of meditation deities and mandalas sit on the table top below with my silver offering bowls in front of them. An embroidered wall hanging of a four-sided vajra hangs across the front of the shrine.

I drink in the inspiration. Each image is a reminder of a teaching, an experience, an understanding, a mind state. A wealth of wisdom and compassion graces this room. These images represent the whole of the Buddhadharma, a vision both vast and profound. I open my mind and heart, and transform beneath their gaze.

The veil parts.

I simply am.

Everything simply is, as it is.

Time passes. I do not measure it.

A different place and time emerges from the as-it-is-ness. A different me, yet the same; I sit in meditation posture on the ground high above a valley. Gravel covers the sides of the surrounding mountains. A smatter of snow dusts the top, and a village sits on grasslands at the foot of the valley. I recognise the place, though in this life, I don't know its name, just that I'm in Tibet outside a cave.

A man struggles up the path towards me—my patron with his supplies. A good man, simple but clear in his beliefs. He knows without a doubt the value of his support. He has no time to practise, so he supports me, and I practise for him. Every step I take towards enlightenment, I take for him as well. Did I say he was simple? No, he is wise. He has me do the hard work for him.

This other place and time is like an overlay on my present. I am both this grimy Tibetan yogi and this modern writer half a world and heavens only knows how many years apart. I am here and I am there, and there is not the slightest conflict. I sense that I am many other places as well; in worlds within worlds in a multiverse vaster than any can imagine.

I suspect that my mind has latched onto the view from the Tibetan mountain across the broad valley topped by an endless blue sky because it is symbolic of my present mind state, and the yogi who watches the man draw closer knows that mind state intimately. His accumulated practice makes it easy for me to slip into that vast space. I know it. It is like coming home.

The glimpse dissolves, but the yogi's mind is always with me.

Do no harm: precept one.

Always help: precept two.

Train your mind: precept three. Get this one together and the others are a cinch.

'You may be doing more harm than good,' Sally had said on the day she'd warned me not to write reviews.

'Goodness does not always look like goodness,' I had replied.

'It depends whose side you're looking from,' she'd said in a rare display of insight.

I visualise Dita as best I can. I have no idea what he looks like—his gravatar is a dog. Mine is Merlin—

so I see him as a kind of generic human-shaped blob. I fill the blob with all his anger, pain and frustration, all his shattered hopes and dreams—the ones I shattered with my truth. It manifests as black smoke swirling in the form. The poor man is filled with it.

How painful it must be to live in a mind filled with hate and the desire for vengeance. I want to help him; I really do. I'm not sorry that I wrote the review—he did ask me for it—but I'm sorry he's taken it so badly. There is no need for him to suffer in this way.

Inhale: the black smoke curls into my heart centre and dissolves into the space of love that resides there.

Exhale: a stream of healing white light flows from my heart into Dita and floods him with a love so profound that it washes away his misery and fills him with hope.

Over and over, I repeat the tonglen prayer, like an air conditioner removing the stifling heat and replacing it with refreshing cool air. He may not be able to feel it, but I know that, on some subtle level, it does have an effect.

After a while, I add to my visualisation all the other authors who feel the same way, then all the people in the world who feel the same way, then all the people in the world who don't feel the same way, and then all those who are suffering in any way at all. I think of Tibet, of Syria, Afghanistan, Iraq, the Sudan and so on, and my visualisation is filled to overflowing; the people fade into dots, spreading endlessly around me.

I breathe in their suffering and send back peace, love and happiness.

Then I dissolve the visuals and rest in the knowledge that they have all found some measure of peace. As have I. I can get back to work now.

I know why I don't want to go to Tibet. It would break my heart to see it now.

5

Kelee's World

Voices. Slade's mellow tones and the thin, wobbly voice of the stable master drifted across the courtyard. Kelee looked up from her reading and smiled. The grooms had arrived for work.

Without conscious thought, she found herself at the window again. Her body had a mind of its own when it came to Slade. She feasted on the sight of his strong shoulders and slender hips. Even groomsmen wore swords, and this one would have the wand of a magician tucked in his belt as well. She envied him his tutor in the magical arts; the masters only ever took on those with natural talent, like Kestril. Her brother's illusions were perhaps the best in all of Minion Hills—the high granite peaks and deep forested gullies that were the home to the Magan clans.

Kelee fared better with the sword than the wand, but herbs were her true ally in the endless bid for power that drove Magan society. Her tutor, Miramar, was a master of the healing arts, the best in all of Minion Hills. That was why her father, Lord Menhir, had permitted the Warrior Clan woman to be Kelee's mentor. He didn't know she had opened Kelee's mind to Warrior lore forbidden to the Mage Clans since the formation of their alliance.

The wheelbarrow trundled from the stables, pushed by Slade's strong arms. Even with a stinking load of horse manure before him, the boy smiled and whistled a tune. Kelee suspected that he learnt more than magic from his tutor, or at least from someone, for he had the mental fortitude of a Warrior Clan Magan, another reason why she had found the book Miramar had suggested she read.

She returned to the table, took her seat and rested her gaze on the open page once more. In the old world, before the clans split, every Magan learnt the skills for defeating the demons that now wandered their streets so freely. The black fluid creatures that glided through Menhir Village were rarely seen in the Village of Minion Hills where Miramar lived. Though neutral territory where trade prospered freely, the Warrior Clans kept the beasts at bay there.

Kelee admired the composure of the Warrior Magans and was determined to make that power her own. But her studies had to be done in secret, and time this morning was running out. It would be another hour before Slade would be free to go riding, but her mother could rise at any time, and someone had hidden this book well.

6

Worlds Within Worlds

I wonder if, when revealed, the contents of the book Kelee is reading will delight my metaphysical curiosity, but a quick scan ahead on the manuscript shows that the author isn't about to tell us. My curiosity will have to remain unsatisfied for a while.

Glimpsed through the words on my computer screen, Kelee's world is like a world within a world within my world. How real is it, I wonder, with its talk of swords and magic? Undoubtedly, it exists within the mind of the author, and her words are a gateway for others to enter. Kelee is real to me already. Though she is mere symbols on a screen, I feel as if she exists somewhere.

I turn my head and gaze though the window beside my desk. Clouds roll in from the south, narrowing my view of the blue sky above the treetops. My veggie garden spreads beneath the stately eucalyptus trees. Once vibrant, it suffers now from the same back that makes me suffer. Bending for long periods can have serious repercussions. I take a deep breath and exhale slowly. I don't want to feel so … old.

The veil parts once more, revealing the luminous basis of our world. Tension I didn't know was there eases from my neck and shoulders, and thoughts flee with my breath, leaving pure awareness.

In this state everything exists, the tangible and the intangible together. The world beyond the veil is vast enough to hold all the riches of human imagination. I sense countless worlds, though I cannot see or touch any but my own, but I feel that if I could just shift the frequency to which my mind is tuned, I could enter another.

Kelee's world is out there somewhere, or perhaps I should say, in here. How could it possibly not exist somewhere when the author has sensed it so clearly? Did she create it with her imagination, or did her imagination allow her to find Kelee and her world?

Sometimes, I think too much.

I remember my vow to remain in a pure mind state and let the thoughts go. Keeping the veil open, I turn my attention back to my desk. The polished wood gleams at me through the gaps between the papers strewn across it. I sit taller in my ergonomic office chair; I bet Kelee doesn't have anything other than a cushion to soften the solid wooden chair she would be sitting on at her desk within the granite walls of the Menhir library. I imagine a patterned rug on the flagstone floor, its colours muted with age, and rows of books in shelves reaching to the ceiling, each novel a world within that world within my world.

Is the world I see in my imagination the same as the one the author sees? Or do I create another world with my extrapolations from the glimpses she gives me?

If every reader creates a new world, then from this one story arises a world for every reader. I find it easier to believe that Kelee's world already exists and the author's words are the portal to take us there. But that is purely conjecture. Fictional worlds are not real—are they?

Merlin jumps onto my desk, strides over to my computer and plonks himself on the keyboard. Way to bring me back to this world, cat!

He purrs, as if I should be happy for the interruption. I give his silky fur a quick stroke, then remove him from my keyboard and dump him on his cushion on the side of my desk. I manage to get one paragraph dealt with before he comes back and adds his opinion to the manuscript. Xcbjkfnjb.

Deep.

He rubs his jaw against mine while I reach around him to edit the next paragraph, but ignoring him is not acceptable—to him. He wanders onto the keyboard again. I take him off. He walks back and stares into my eyes.

'Fine,' I mutter and slide open my top drawer. I extract a white catnip mouse and throw it over my shoulder. 'Get the mouse, Merlin. Get the mouse!'

He obliges by leaping off my desk and racing after it. I watch him bat the thing around, amazed at the dexterity of his paws as he picks it up, throws it in the air and catches it again. He tumbles over it in a forward roll, holds it with his front paws and kicks at it with his back. I chuckle.

Thanks for the laugh, Merlin.

I wiggle an old fabric belt in front of him and smile while he bats at it, then kicks and gnaws it in rapid succession. His pupils dilate and his eyes take on that manic look. I wonder how he sees the world we share. Does he see beings that humans don't?

That's one thing I expect I'll never know. I wrap the belt around him and leave him chewing on it.

7

Party

I'm really bad at this.

I look around the room at all the people in little groups talking and laughing. It seems that everyone has someone, except me. Most appear to be couples. Not surprising, I suppose, since this is an engagement party for Liz's little sister who is, being in her twenties, right at the marrying kind of age, along with her friends. Thirty-three and still single makes me the odd one out. Not that it bothers me.

'Your biological clock is ticking,' Liz, my best friend, had told me when I'd returned from my three years in a retreat centre in the south of France, and she'd been dragging me off to various social activities ever since. Was I hoping I'd find someone? Perhaps just a little, but not enough to make me disappointed that not one person of the male variety interests me in this sea of faces.

The mix of voices, high-pitched laughter and thumping music assaults my aural sense. I'm not used to the alcohol either, which makes me a little woozy, but Liz shoved a glass in my hand when I arrived and it gives me something to hang onto while I hold up the wall and wish they'd play some decent music. No one's dancing anyway, and I have more room and a better sound system at home, but these people would probably think me crazy for dancing alone. Not that I care.

I'm wasting my time here. I'd be better off working on the book.

An old matron turns from her conversation and eyes my spiky, blue-tipped white-blonde hair through narrowed eyes. I send her a smile and she quickly looks away.

Sheesh. Do I look that dangerous? I look down. Fair enough. I am wearing my demon-kicking boots, all studs and spikes; and my black jacket and jeans finish off the tough girl look. Liz said I could've dressed a little more approachable—and she'd made it sound like I should have. But at least I'm here. If anyone's willing to broach the defences, they might just be worth knowing.

I'm about to head to the door when I feel someone's gaze beaming across the room at me. I turn to the source. A pair of clear eyes look at me from behind a group of laughing teens. Our gaze meets, and a smile blossoms on a well-proportioned face. I feel a kindred spirit and can't help smiling. He steps towards me at the same time as a tacky, but very popular, dance track starts up, and couples flood the space in the centre of the room. The mystery man disappears behind clusters of gyrating bodies. I try to locate him, but someone steps in front of me. A man, but not the one I wanted.

He eyes my naked ring finger, then smiles and shouts over the music. 'Hi. Name's Scott. Wanna dance?'

Where did he come from? I frown and consider the proposal while he waits, looking slightly annoyed that I even had to think about it. 'I don't like the music,' I shout back. 'And there's no space.'

'I'll take that as a 'no', then.' At least that's what I think he says. It could have been, *so you're a little bit slow then.* And he could have been right.

Liz would kill me if I turned down such an offer, and the guy looks decent, though in a kind of too smooth way: broad face, pale, deep-set eyes, thin lips, and not much of a chin, and he's combed his dark hair flat against his head. The overall effect is reasonably pleasant, however. 'Maybe later with a different track.'

Someone turns the music up, and I lose his next words, but he gestures to the food table while his mouth moves like a fish out of water—blub, blub, burble, burble. I nod and surreptitiously check him out as I follow him to the spread laid out in the next room. He has broad shoulders and seems well built beneath his jacket, but when he turns towards me, I note a softening around his gut and the beginning of jowls.

The volume in the dining room is somewhat more conducive to conversation, but I yearn for the silence of home, or at least the depth and purity of the music that inspires me—far too theatrical for most people. I grab a mini meat pie, dip it in tomato sauce and take a bite, surprised at how hungry I am. Hopefully, it will soak up the alcohol.

'Pretty disgusting spread,' he says, peering over the offerings with a look of disdain.

'Oh, come on, you can't beat party pies and sausage rolls,' I say, selecting one that still looks hot.

'Really.' He looks quite pained as I stuff it in my mouth and moan in pleasure. The traditional Aussie party food had accompanied every birthday party I'd ever had. It evokes fond memories of a hard-working and loving mum. I wipe a tear aside. The house she'd left me had brought me home from Sydney.

Scott finds an acceptable mini quiche and pulls a condescending face as he eats it.

'You new here?' I ask.

He nods. 'Staying in the motel down the road for a couple of weeks, but I might stay longer; it's nice here.'

'You a Sydneyite, then?'

He nods.

'Do I detect a touch of American in your accent?' I ask.

'I spent my high school years there,' he replies, then jerks his head in the direction of the main room. 'You ready for that dance now?'

A reasonably decent track plays, so I nod. 'One dance, then I'm going home,' I say, just so he doesn't get his hopes up.

I dutifully give him his dance, but my eyes look pretty much everywhere other than him while we dance—somewhat awkwardly on his part—and I do glimpse the mystery man once again—but only once. We exchange another smile, and he takes a step in my direction until his gaze rests on Scott, who moves in just a little too close at that exact moment. By the time I step back, mystery man has disappeared, and I don't see him again.

Scott tries to convince me to stay and tags along when I find Liz to say goodbye. She eyes him off, then gives me a good-one-girl look and follows me to the loo, where I discover that she's never seen him before and suspects him of gatecrashing.

'What's it matter? He looks quite eligible,' she says while she runs her fingers through her long brown hair and purses her lips at the mirror.

I want to ask her who the other guy is, but realise that I haven't seen enough of him to be able to give a description, so I give up on that idea and rush off before Scott can ask for my phone number. Kiama is a small town. If it's meant to happen I'll see him again.

8

Walk

My hamstrings strain with a sudden burst of speed. Merlin races ahead and I sprint after him, determined to let him have a good run before he gets to the end of his leash and must yank to a stop—there's too many snakes, foxes and paralysing ticks up here, and too many beautiful birds I don't want him to kill for me to let him run wild. My heart is pounding now, and I wish I was as fit as I was when I danced eight hours a day.

He leaps up the rock, paws scrabbling at the top as he fights to pull himself over the edge. He makes it—he always does—then sits above me, looking down with his head cocked, his bright eyes telling me how clever he is.

'Yes, you're a clever boy,' I say.

He licks a paw, then runs it over his face and behind his ear, and I lean against the rock to catch my breath. By the time I climb up beside him, he's sitting still, listening. I sit without moving and listen with him. I hear with the ears of a cat, see through the eyes of a cat, and my nose twitches as it sifts the smells for information.

Something dead and decaying to the north; damp earth and leaf mulch to the east; dry rock and lichen below, and the perfume of eucalyptus blossoms dances on the breeze.

The sounds of the rainforest leap forth like crystal bells ringing in the silence of a grand cathedral. Birdsong punctuates the background texture of cicadas buzzing in the trees: a lyre bird, a cat bird, native wrens, finches and thrush, and far away the call of a currawong. The names do not matter to a cat, and right now, they don't matter to me either.

Leaves rustle; we turn to the sound. Something large is hiding behind a shrub. Merlin crouches on his haunches, ready to pounce, his gaze, filled with anticipation, fixed on the movement. It doesn't matter to him that whatever is there is clearly as tall as a man. He's just interested in the hunt.

Like Dita.

I curse my human brain for drawing a computer world character into my physical reality, and I bring my mind back to what I see. I return to the present and just look, without mental commentary. The tension imported with the memory of Dita fades.

The glossy, green leaves of the bush are still now. Whatever it is waits. Merlin creeps along the rock on his belly, his nose twitching, tail flipping back and forth. What does he smell? I hope it's just a large wallaby or a roo. Could it be a man?

A man like Dita?

Though he hunts on the internet, someone is behind the name, someone who lives somewhere. My chest contracts.

Don't be ridiculous.

There is no way he could be here. But if he was, does he hate me enough to knife me, or shoot me? It's unlikely, but there are lots of crazy people in the world. I realise that if I don't stop the growing paranoia, I'll be one of them. I jump off the rock. 'Come on, Merlin, let's go.'

Thump, thump, thump. I catch a glimpse of a large wallaby fleeing through the forest. My mind created the fear, nothing more. It was never real.

Merlin casts one look after his prey, decides it's a lost cause and ambles on. A finch flutters past, catching his attention. He races after it, taking up the full length of his leash, then simply stands and watches as the bird flies out of reach. The wallaby is forgotten, relegated to a past that no longer exists. I put Dita in the same place and run my gaze up the broad trunk before me.

Thousands of insects dwell between and beneath the rough bark, their world crowned by silver green leaves dancing against the backdrop of a brilliant, blue sky. I stare into the sky and smile. I will not give Dita the satisfaction of allowing him to disturb a moment like this. I'm back where I belong, on the right side of the veil.

9

Kelee's World

Hooves pounded the earth, churning up clods of dirt softened by the night's rain. Kelee galloped her white mare after Slade, and the stonewalled houses of Menhir Village faded into the distance behind her. He hooted back to her from his bay. 'You'll not catch me this day!'

Kelee gritted her teeth and tossed her black hair off her face, wishing she had bound it. But Slade liked it flowing free, and now it streamed out behind her, dancing in the cool breeze that kissed her cheeks.

The forest drew close fast. Slade was right, Kelee thought; she would never catch him now, not on Flake. The mare's strength was beauty, not speed.

Slade reined in Knox at the edge of the forest and turned, grinning, as Kelee rode up beside him.

'It's the horse, not the rider,' she said. 'You know that, don't you?' Kelee only won a race against the groom when she rode Kestril's black stallion, Pitch.

'Of course, Miss, whatever you say, Miss.' He laughed, the hearty full-throated laugh that she loved.

She reached over and poked him on the arm with her crop. He knew she hated it when he reminded her of their difference in station.

'Argh.' He clutched his arm in mock horror, slid off the horse as if she'd knocked him from his seat and rolled on the ground moaning.

She dismounted and stood over him, hands on hips, mouth twisted, shaking her head at his antics. He grabbed her calf and pulled her down beside him. His lips found hers, and their arms and legs tangled. For those blissful moments, nothing else in the world mattered. His woodsy smell, his soft lips, his warm hands and firm chest filled her senses—until the sound of hooves cantering along the woodland path had her flinging herself apart from him, terrified that someone would see them. She scrambled to her feet and stood panting, eyes wide, staring into the forest until the sound faded away.

He sat up. 'They were going too fast. They never would have seen us.' She heard the hurt in his voice and saw the sadness in his eyes.

'Beak has spies everywhere. All he needs is one of them to see us, and I'm busted—well and truly.'

He stood and brushed the grass from his trousers. 'Your father would forgive you. He's a tough man, but he's also fair, and he loves his beautiful little girl.'

Kelee shrugged. 'He wouldn't stop Beak declaring a duel, though.'

Slade's eyebrows rose. 'To save your honour?'

'He said he'd kill you if he found us together.' Kelee slid her fingers through Flake's bridle and turned her towards the forest.

'Wait!'

She looked back and winced at the hurt in his voice.

'You think I couldn't beat him?'

'I don't know, but I don't want to risk it.'

'I may only be a groom, but I have some tricks up my sleeve, especially if I had to prove I was good enough for you.'

Kelee smiled. 'You are good enough for me. Beak is half the man you are. He wants me as a possession, a trophy, but you love me. Mother would see that.'

'And that's why we should tell her.'

'No!'

He recoiled at her tone. Her voice had sounded harder than she intended. 'I couldn't bear it if they forbade me to see you,' she explained, willing him to understand. They couldn't let anything jeopardise what they had. She feared she would lose it all too soon.

He simply nodded and, schooling his expression into the impassive mask worn by Magan men, walked his horse into the forest. She trailed behind him, ducking the branches until they found the trail. Then they remounted and continued at a trot.

The path was not wide enough for two abreast, so Kelee followed Slade, and neither spoke. A heaviness had settled upon them, made more ominous by the dim light imposed by the thick canopy. The feeling in this part of the thick forest that covered most of Minion Hills reminded Kelee of that in the Morbid Forest, as if the trees mourned for something lost, or was it just her mourning for a love bound to fall to social expectations?

Even here, they had to duck the occasional low branch or dangling creeper, testament to the lack of traffic on the path. She wondered who had passed before in such a hurry—someone else who didn't want to be seen? Kelee sighed. Why shouldn't she and Slade have a future together? Love should be more important than political alliances.

Kestril had insinuated that things would change when he became Lord of the Menhirs. Would he be her ally in this? She hardly knew her secretive brother, but did his skills as an illusionist extend to turning a groom into a nobleman? Even he couldn't do that.

Slade turned off the woodland path into a narrow track so overgrown that they soon had to dismount and walk the horses. The track ascended gradually at first, then more steeply, and the trees grew fewer and more scraggly when the ground turned from clay to granite. Dappled sunshine broke through the thinned canopy and the atmosphere brightened. Kelee vowed not to say anything that would spoil their time together.

Voices. They grew louder as Kelee and Slade drew nearer to their destination. Someone else knew of their private place. They hid the horses off the track behind a wall of shrubs and, curious, crept closer.

'Feed me first, then perhaps we will have a deal.'

Kelee and Slade exchanged horrified glances. The thin, icy voice could only belong to a Rasa demon. The things gave both of them the creeps, and they stayed out of their way as much as possible. Most villagers, too powerless to stop them, tolerated their feeding, and some—always the most angry, lustful, jealous, prejudiced or just plain dull-witted of the clan—fed them willingly, as if they were pets. But no one was supposed to strike a deal with one. Everyone knew how dangerous that was.

Though Kelee figured they should have turned in the other direction, she and Slade tiptoed even closer, lured by the prospect of knowing the identity of one who dealt with demons. They stopped behind a bush leafy enough to keep them from view, but flexible enough for them to bend the branches back and peek through.

Kelee had to stifle a gasp. Beak stood with his head titled to the side, exposing his neck to a huge red-eyed demon. Its black flowing skin hung off it like the drapery of a hooded cloak. The demon's eyes flamed with pleasure, and liquid fire dripped from his slit of a mouth like drool. The long talon on his right hand rested on Beak's neck. His glazed eyes stared into space and a sleazy grin twisted his face. He began to pant, his breath quickening, and his hands caressed some form seen only by him. He clasped the invisible form to his chest and thrust his hips as if ...

Kelee grimaced. Beak's trousers bulged at the front. It wasn't hard to imagine what fantasy fed this demon.

'Kelee,' Beak moaned. 'Oooh, Kelee.' His hips thrust harder and faster.

Kelee twisted away from the sight, her stomach heaving. The bastard! How dare he! She took a step deeper into the forest, but Slade grabbed her arm and placed a finger to his lips, then he wrapped an arm around her and pulled her into his embrace. She buried her face in his chest and tried to shut out Beak's moans.

Eventually, the demon spoke again. 'I will fire her desires and fill her fantasies with your face. You will feed me again in two days.'

'Deal.' Beak's voice came out huskier than usual; it revolted Kelee even more.

Slade lowered them both quietly to the ground and they lay still until the sounds of Beak riding away had faded into the distance.

The demon sniffed, then rollicked with cruel laughter. 'The ground is fertile, little one,' he mocked. 'I will come for you soon. And I suggest that you submit gracefully. Your lover cannot survive what your incestuous cousin has in store for him.'

Kelee stared at Slade with wide, wet eyes, and the sound of the demon's laughter diminished as the beast disappeared into the forest on the other side of the clearing. They moved only when the forest had returned to its usual stillness.

The beast knew I was here, Kelee thought, feeling invaded already.

Slade put a hand on each of her shoulders and looked into her eyes with an earnest gaze. 'You need to talk to Miramar. She will know how to protect you from the demon.'

'And Beak?' she whispered. 'Can she protect me from him as well?'

'I'll take care of him.'

Kelee struggled to her feet on quivering legs. But who would protect Slade?

10

Unfriend

Phew. Intense concentration on that scene. I check my Facebook. Mostly the usual: gorgeous cat memes; inspirational and political messages; and posts and photos by my friends on various aspects of their lives.

My notifications inform me that Dita has mentioned me in a status update. A feeling of trepidation stirs in my gut as I click through. If he still feels the way he did when he wrote that email, I'm not expecting this to be good. It isn't.

Prunella Smith is a dyke bitch who spends her life finding ways to emasculate every man she comes across. I reckon she's part of that 'review mafia' that gangs up on self-published authors and bullies them until they crawl into a corner and cry. Well, I'm not crying. I'm fighting back.

A dyke bitch? Seriously. *A bully?* Me? He's the bully! I stare in disbelief, shake my head and blink a few times before I come to my senses.

Since when have I cared what others think?

It still hurts.

He wanted me to see it—that's why he put the link to my name. Vindictive bastard.

For a moment, I wonder why I ever accepted his friend request, then I remember how nice and supportive his regular comments on my blog had been. Had he just been buttering me up, getting me onside for a positive review right from the beginning? If so, his strategy failed. Still, I feel somewhat played, and a little stupid. I invited a viper into my nest.

My first instinct is to say something rude back, but I don't—sometimes it's hard being a Buddhist. It would only inflame him further anyway. I note with satisfaction that a few of my friends have defended me, but others—clearly not my friends—have happily joined the slander bandwagon. Shit draws flies and breeds maggots. Negativity breeds negativity. Luckily, the opposite is also true.

I click on the little down-facing arrow thing and view my options:

I don't want to see this
Report this post
Unfollow Dita

That pretty much sums up my feelings, but I only get one click. I decide on *Report this post* and am surprised that there isn't a bullying option on their next list.

Why don't you want to see this:
It's annoying or not interesting
I don't think it should be on Facebook
It's spam

I go for the top one, then, to make sure I don't see anything from him in my News Feed ever again, I go to my friends list, find the 'Unfriend' button and make that my friend by removing a few 'friends' from my list—fiends not friends; they never deserved the 'r' after the 'f'. I snigger at how simple it is. Click a button and declare someone your friend; click another button and they're not your friend anymore—kind of makes the whole idea of friend and not-friend somewhat arbitrary. Just as the Buddhadharma says.

The idea is to move fast. I make sure I do everything I can to shut him out of my feed and out of my mind.

Of course, I can't really stop him saying whatever he likes about me, but at least I don't have to look at it anymore. I hope this is the end of it.

It isn't.

I have a quick scan of my emails and find that someone commented on a topic I'm following on a blog. I click through to the blog and my heart sinks as I read the new comment.

Ella Smith is one of those bully reviewers. She visciously attacked my work in an attempt to destroy my livelihood. Semi-illeterate vindictive people like her shouldn't be allowed to write reviews. Her own book looks like it was written by someone in a remedial english class.

It's Dita. The bastard is stalking me! And calling me semi-illiterate when he can't even spell the word, or put a capital on English.

My hurt rapidly morphs into anger—the dangerous, self-righteous kind. My teeth clench without my permission, and I have to consciously relax my muscles.

I try to make light of it—*visciously attacked? Semi-illeterate? english?*—but his errors bring little comfort.

I'm not going to let this go on.

After a few deep breaths and a search for the contact form, I send an email to the owner of the blog and ask if she'll take the comment down. Please. If the vehemence of his language isn't enough, my explanation of his email and Facebook attack should be enough for her to see what's going on.

That took far too much time!

'What else can I do?' I ask Merlin, who's pacing back and forth by the door.

Bite the bastard.

I grimace. Hardly the non-violent approach.

The cat shoots me a disdainful look. *You did ask.*

Yeah.

I need to get back to work, but I can't settle, and the fact that I can't settle reminds me of the reason. Dita's abuse runs loops in my head, and each repeat makes me madder. I stare out the window and try to slip through the veil to safety, but I can't even find the entrance. I'm trapped in my neurotic mind. Not only has he wasted my time, he's blocking my ability to live in the world of my choice.

This is not real, I remind myself before my mental gymnastics muddy my mind further. It's only pixels on a screen. None of it is real. I slap my thigh— that is real.

11

Liz

After spending the rest of the morning focused on my editing job, I head off to the local village. I'd tried to get out of my weekly get-together with Liz, but she'd insisted that no matter how stretched I was for time, I needed to get out further than the forest at the bottom of my garden. Since I'd tucked a good few thousand words under my belt and had to get some groceries anyway, I agreed.

I drive out of the valley with the usual strange feeling that I'm leaving a place of magic and entering the ordinary world. Truth is, I am. The forest gives way to fields and the fields to houses as I drive along the narrow road down the hill and along the valley floor. At the T-intersection with the busy highway, I wait for a gap then pull into the stream of traffic.

My best friend lives in a double-brick house with a double garage and a double-chinned mother in law, who lives in a double-room granny flat out the back. I park on the street, slide out of the car and follow the petunia-lined path around the side. I clatter through the gate into the backyard, and the youngest, Amy, who's making mud pies in the sand pit, stops and looks up. She gives me a toothless grin and wipes some bedraggled red curls off her face, leaving a scour of grit.

'Hi, Amy. How's things?'

She just shrugs and goes back to her game. I open the screen door at the back of the house and poke my head inside. 'Yoo hoo, Liz,' I call.

She bounds out of the kitchen, thick strawberry-blond hair bouncing around her shoulders, and rushes over to me with her arms wide. I grin and step through the door and into her embrace.

'So good to see you,' she says, then she pulls back, holds me by the upper arm and tilts her head, sizing me up like some maiden aunt.

'Hi, Aunt Ella,' Amy chimes. The screen door bangs behind her.

Oh, yeah, that's right; I'm the maiden aunt! Actually, I'm the kid's godmother, but you get the idea.

Liz nods and releases me, apparently satisfied with what she sees. 'The kettle's just boiled; what do you want?' She leads the way into the kitchen.

'Coffee will be fine,' I say as I follow.

We share the usual greetings, then take our drinks to the back deck so we can keep an eye on Amy, who now has several brightly coloured plastic ponies in the sandpit. She eyes the plate of cookies Liz sets on the white plastic table.

'Girls with sick tummies don't get biscuits,' Liz says.

Amy twists her little face into a knot and huffs.

'I'm not sure just how sick that tummy is, but I figure if she needs a day off school, she probably does need one.'

I nod in agreement. Liz is as solid as her frame, as generous as her curves and as caring as her kind eyes suggest.

'So, what's ruffled your feathers?' she asks.

'I'm not ruffled!'

'The hell you are, girl. I heard it in your voice on the phone.'

She would know. She's been my friend since primary school. 'Fine. I think I'm being cyber-bullied.'

Her jaw drops. 'You think?'

I sigh in resignation. I do not want to be a victim. 'Yeah.'

She leans back in her chair, folds her arms and lowers her chin with an okay-spill-it look on her face, so I tell her all about Dita and what I've done in response to his attacks.

'And this has all happened today?'

'Yep. I posted the review yesterday.'

Liz whistles slowly. 'Sounds like you've done the right thing. But you're not going to let it bug you, are you?'

'Me? No way.'

She raises an eyebrow and purses her lips as if to say, go on, tell me another one.

'Okay, fine. It pisses me off. I can let it go, but it comes back whenever I think of how … unfair it all is.'

She nods. 'You've a right to be pissed off. The guy's a jerk.'

I shake my head.

'What?' she asks, eyes all innocent. 'He is.'

I nod and chuckle. Liz is such a good reality check. She's so grounded, she's like Mother Earth herself. 'Yeah, he is, but thinking like that doesn't help me.'

She smiles. 'I know, hon, but you have to let yourself say what you're feeling, acknowledge it first, then let it go. You gotta shout a bit first. It does you no good to hold it in.'

I nod and don't even try to explain that I don't hold in; I let go. They probably look the same to her anyway. All she sees is that I'm not grumbling where grumbling's warranted. And perhaps she's right. Maybe I do need to indulge in a good grumble. I just don't want to solidify the situation in my mind.

'Feel it, then let it go.' She spits my words from several months ago back at me with a grin.

'Fine.'

The conversation then dissolves into a slanging match where we do all the slanging, hurling as many derogatory terms as we can at the grumpy author on the other side of the world. When we finally collapse into giggles with tears running down our faces, Amy wanders over, tilts her head, just like her mum does, and says, 'What's so funny?'

We crack up even more at that. How can we tell a six-year-old that we just called someone a limp penis with bad breath and a foreskin five sizes too big. No way could his little tiny thing ever fill its great big over-coat!

'Nothing, honey,' Liz says, wiping her eyes.

'I think we should talk about something else,' I say. 'But thanks, I feel much better.'

'Nothing like a good laugh to soothe the soul,' Liz says and wipes Amy's snotty nose. I can't help screwing up my nose just a little.

'Pah,' she says, catching my expression, 'just wait a couple of years, you'll see. They'll start to look real cute.'

I stand and stretch my arms above my head while Liz gives her daughter some motherly attention. I've never wanted kids, been too busy dancing to even think of that kind of thing, even with Tom. I still feel the jolt of disappointment at how that ended, or rather at the fact that it ended at all. I'd thought he was the love of my life, but when my back became a major issue and I couldn't stay with the ballet company, he still went to America—without me.

'I'd always imagined you and me in the lead roles,' he'd said when he broke up with me. 'But that's never going to happen now, and I don't want to stop it from happening with someone else.'

He'd wanted us to be Nureyev and Fonteyn, but when I couldn't lift my leg that high without back pain, he decided that finding a new Fonteyn for his Nureyev was more important than a relationship with me. He'd broken my heart, and I'd felt foolish that I'd thought we'd had something special. How could I have got it so wrong? Is it any wonder that I didn't want to put myself in that situation again? After that trauma, all I wanted was peace in my life, but now … Liz is right. The clock is ticking.

I wander over to look at her collection of garden ornaments. A variety of mushrooms with assorted tops, rocks with eyes and mouths, and funny little creatures she calls bunyips cluster around the steps onto the deck. She even has a couple of gumnut babies. I haven't seen them before. 'Started a new series, have you?'

'Yeah. The tourists like the cutesy ones, so I've bowed to pressure. They put the fees up on the stalls again, and no one buys the big stuff, but they'll pay for something cute; so cute's the new look.'

I understand all too well. At least my books can travel the world in ebook form. Liz can only sell to those who visit the local market once a month or who order from her website—and few do; postage is expensive and tricky.

'I can't stop making these, though,' she adds.

I turn and follow her proud gaze. An unglazed terracotta mask hangs on the outside wall of the house. Shells adorn hair that flows in a halo around a face that's both beautiful and terrible. 'A mermaid?'

She shakes her head. 'A siren. Much more dangerous.'

I nod appreciatively. I'm amazed at how she gets such a fine expression in clay. 'It's stunning.'

'Yeah, I think so.' She nods with satisfaction, and I can see that, despite her frustration at a world which likes to enjoy art but never pay for it, she's happy. Kevin brings in a fat pay cheque each week and loves her and her work. So long as he's there to pay the bills, she can indulge in her art, and who knows … maybe one day she'll be discovered. Neither of us hang out for that event any more though.

'So, that guy, what was his name?' she says as Amy runs past, back to her grimy game.

'Who?'

'The party, remember?'

'Oh, him.' I sit back at the table and cross my legs. 'Scott, I think it was. What about him?'

'Have you heard from him?'

'No, why should I?'

She jiggles in her seat like a twelve-year-old with a secret.

'You didn't,' I say, knowing full well that she must have.

She nods. 'He asked if I had it, so I gave it to him. Can't hurt.'

'I don't know anything about him.'

She scooped some crumbs from the table and dropped them back onto the biscuit plate. 'And you won't get to know him unless you see him again. Which you won't, unless a friend with your best interests at heart gives him your phone number.'

'Thanks, but …'

'What?'

'I'm not sure he's right for me.'

'God, girl, you'll never know if you don't give him a chance. You can't just keep on staying up there all alone. You'll turn into a crazy cat lady. I mean, who do you see apart from me?'

I shrug. She knows the answer. I'm not good at cultivating friends. I do all right by myself. 'I'm not going out chasing men,' I say and get rolled eyes for my trouble. I agree that the refrain is starting to sound a little hollow. I never will chase them—it's just not me—but she does have a point. Do I want to miss out on the cosy kind of partnership Liz shares with Kevin, that my mum shared with my dad?

'You don't have to chase them; just be available, and say yes when they call.'

'Okay.'

'And get out more.'

'Yeah.'

'Wanna come to the market with me next time?'

I nod. 'Sure. So long as I can bring my laptop.' I can't risk making my editing client wait for her book.

12

Crusader

An email from Sally, my publisher's marketing manager, awaits my attention:

Do you know this person? It sounds like you've reviewed his book.

Uh, oh. This doesn't sound good.

I follow her link to the Amazon product page for my book, *Catnip Creek*. A lone one star review stands out like a beacon down the bottom of the bar graph that shows the numbers of reviews for each star rating. I click on it. Someone calling themselves VP Obber (very pissed off?) has written:

Catnip Creek is without a doubt the worst book I've ever read. The author can't write, yet she writes reviews of other people's books. Her negative reviews are just because she's jealous and she wants to put down the competition. This stupid book is about this old couple and their stupid cat, and no one really cares about them. I'd give it minus five stars if that was possible, but since I can't, and I can't give it no stars, I'll be generous and give her one star.

I stare at my computer screen, amazed by the tenacity of my cyber-stalker. I care about Carl and Clarrisa! A sick feeling fills my stomach; I don't like feeling so powerless, and I have no control over this, no way to prevent it happening again, and though they're just words, they do have power—for anyone who chooses to believe them. I take a deep breath and remember that I do have control over my mind. On the exhalation, I raise my eyes and fix on the photo of my lama pinned to the noticeboard above my desk. A memory of his presence washes over me and chases my upset away. It may not look like it, but I've won this round.

I've reported it as inappropriate, Sally has written. *Hopefully, the friendly giant will recognise it for what it is and remove it.*

Thanks, I type and hit *Send*. I click on the *Report it as Inappropriate* button as well, but I don't have her faith in the 'friendly giant'. Amazon won't take the review down unless it contravenes their policy and I don't think this does. At least Sally didn't say, 'I told you so'.

I remember the nasal tones of her Sydney accent on the phone when she warned me:

'I know it's your own business, darling, but it's just safer today if authors don't write reviews. You should be writing your next book, not reading others, especially if they're crap.'

'I don't finish them if they're crap.'

'Good for you. You wouldn't believe how many manuscripts the editors here discard after the first page.'

I snort. 'Oh, yes, I would. Those are the ones I refuse to review at all.'

'Why do you have to read self-published ones anyway?' she said. 'Everyone knows cheap ebooks are just a public slush-pile.'

'That's exactly why.'

'It is? What?' Her baby blues would have widened at that.

'There are real gems out there, Sally, and they don't deserve to be lumped in with the rest.'

'Hmmph. But you don't have to talk about the bad ones. We never do, you know. It only encourages them to argue. The good old rejection slip saves everyone a lot of bother.'

'But I do have to talk about the bad ones,' I'd replied, 'because hardly anyone else does, so there's all these books out there without a single bad review, not because the book is any good, but because those who read it are too scared, too 'nice', or too lazy to write what they think. And the poor unsuspecting reader ends up with a lemon.'

'All credit to your magnanimous heart, darling. Readers clearly owe you big time.'

I'd gritted my teeth at the sarcasm.

'But seriously, it's a pointless crusade. No one is going to thank you for it, and the market is just too vast for one noble person standing up for the truth to make a difference. And it could make you the target of pissed-off authors, which is why, as your marketing manager, I'm advising you not to write reviews.'

That's why I didn't tell her about Dita.

I put my computer to sleep and take a stretch break. I guess it is a bit of a crusade. I see the headline splashed across some imaginary newspaper: Prunella Smith, author of the whimsical *Catnip Creek*, single-handedly takes on the task of bringing real critical appraisal to self-published books.

Is that what I'm doing?

I shrug. What does it matter what I call it? I'm not going to let anyone bully me into not saying what needs to be said:

Like: YOUR BOOK STINKS.

Or: IT SERIOUSLY SUCKS.

It did; it really did—Dita's book, that is—but I would never say it like that. I wrote a detailed, and very polite and objective summary of how it failed in the areas of plot, character development, dialogue, pacing and prose—not to mention the copy-editing, or lack of it. The review was almost a manuscript appraisal! I charge dollars for them; this guy got it for free and he's got the nerve to ... to ...

My breathing quickens. My jaw tightens. I take a deep breath and exhale slowly to expel the anger. Now I'll have to take a few minutes to clear my head before I can resume work. Precious minutes that I can ill afford to take from my editing time.

Damn.

13

Brush Off

Downward Dog is a strange name for an arrangement of the body. Bum up, head down, arms and legs straight. Imagine someone lifting up your hips ... sttrreeeettcchh. Ahhhh. It feels goood. I bring myself upright, stretch my spine up and arch backwards. Three times and I'm done.

I walk from my studio—polished floorboards, a mirrored wall and a dance barre, all that remains of my life as a dancer—and into my office, ready to start the day. I turn on the computer and stare out the window while everything loads. The misty bush calls to me, and I wonder if the drizzle will stop. The eucalyptus forest that wraps my house in its deep-green embrace is like an addiction. I have to have my regular hit, but it's rained the last few days. Am I willing to take an umbrella and risk leeches to visit the lookout? Probably, but Merlin will have to stay behind. The little ones get between his toes and are hard to get out. I can sprinkle them with salt—then they shrivel up and die— but that isn't exactly sticking to my vow to do no harm.

Nah. It's better he stays here. Besides, he's not that keen on getting his paws wet.

A lyre bird with a full tail of arched feathers is scratching at the bottom of the garden. He's singing, mimicking a bellbird, and his voice really does sound like bells. I love the way it cuts through the stillness with a clarity so powerful that it's almost unreal—super real. I'd like to throw a stick at the bloody great chook. Its huge claws tear up my lawn and make it really hard to mow.

My laptop comes to life, drawing my attention back inside. The grey day casts only a dim light into the room, and the computer screen glows brilliant blue in stark contrast to the wooden desk on which it sits. The light is a magnet for my eyes, the screen a window to another world. I sit down, click an icon and let the screen suck me in.

I'm in my inbox again, a familiar place. Rows of neatly ordered subject lines surround me. I skip over the top of most of them, my gaze tuned to pick out anything important. There it is!

Re: sequel to *Catnip Creek*.

My heart leaps, and I take a moment to remind myself not to fall into hope and fear—hope that my publisher will want a sequel and fear that they won't. A deep breath brings me back to the equanimity I had in my morning meditation. On the deepest, most important layer of reality, it really doesn't matter.

I open the door to this particular room and dive into the words, wondering if those I land on will be soft or spiky. Either way, I could easily turn them soggy. No, I will not cry.

Dear Prunella

We [the impersonal we; not a good start] *like the idea of a sequel very much;* [heart leaps] *however,* [heart sinks—what happened to no hope and fear?] Catnip Creek *has not performed as well as expected. Therefore, we are unable to offer publication of a sequel.*

We wish you the best of luck with your future endeavours as a writer and are sorry that we cannot be of more assistance at this time.

Yours sincerely… blah blah blah.

My heart's in my ugg boots now. Sitting there like a lead weight.

Spiky. Fine. So be it.

I'm not really surprised. I glance up at the photo on the noticeboard above my desk. There's me in the local bookstore pointing to *Catnip Creek* on the shelf. I was so over the moon about that. I figured my career was made. I had a publisher! I never dreamed they would only want one book. And I never dreamed that the book would only just make back the advance they gave me—it wasn't a big one either. *Catnip Creek* disappeared from the shelves even before three months was up and, despite all my online efforts, sales dropped right off. Despite its fans and rave reviews, my début novel just didn't take off.

They didn't even offer to look at a different title, should I ever write one—unlikely now. That last sentence sounded like a big fat goodbye, done, we're finished with you.

Yes. I'm disappointed, but I shrug it off and return to work.

A few minutes later, I realise that I've looked at that same paragraph about four times without actually doing anything to fix the problems. Dita's lurking in the back of my mind, sabotaging my efforts, and for so long as I let him stay there, I am not likely to get the editing done on time. Part of me said I couldn't afford the time to stop and meditate, the other said I couldn't afford not to. The latter won.

14

Kelee's World

Kelee snuggled up to Slade and hoped that Miramar's herbs worked. Apparently they did—mostly. ~~A pregnancy from him wouldn't be totally unwanted though;~~ If the choice were possible, she would choose him to be the father of her children anyway. Perhaps, if she did find herself pregnant with his child, they may allow her to marry him.

She sighed and opened her eyes. The forest closed in around them like a protective cloak, and the leaves made a soft bed beneath their blanket. Would they ever sleep together in a real bed? ~~She wondered.~~

Slade's eyes opened. He turned his head, ~~looked at her~~ [gazed into her eyes] and smiled. 'What's the big sigh for?' ~~he asked~~.

'Just … nothing.'

'Hmm.' He pulled her closer and stroked her hair, clearly not fooled for a moment. 'We'll find a way.'

'I love you. You know that, don't you?'

'Of course, and I love you too.' He rolled onto his side and kissed her gently on her lips. 'But we should go. We can't afford to make anyone suspicious.'

Kelee nodded and sat up. The horses waited patiently nearby, chomping on their bits. Her horse whickered gently, answered by Slade's gelding. They would have preferred to be left grazing in the field instead of hidden in the forest, but ~~had~~ [if] anyone ~~seen~~ [saw] them riderless …

Slade buttoned his fly, and Kelee pulled her underwear on beneath her skirt. Her [choice of] clothing was a secret message to her lover. A skirt meant she had time for love making. [When[ever] she met him for her morning ride dressed the old fashioned way,] he ~~always~~ greeted her with a wide smile and twinkling eyes ~~when she met him for her morning ride dressed the old fashioned way~~.

He stood ~~first~~ and offered her his hand. She grasped it and let him help her to her feet, then stepped aside and smoothed down her embroidered skirt while he folded the blanket.

They untied the horses and led them through the undergrowth. Close to the field where light ~~was filtering~~ filtered into the forest ~~from the open field when,~~ they heard ~~it—the pounding of~~ horses' hooves trotting, then galloping ~~and fading~~ into the distance. Kelee gasped, and turned to Slade with wide eyes.

He met her look with a frown. 'We'll take the shortcut to the well, then double back; it'll look like we took the long path.'

Kelee nodded. Had the rider been spying on them? A terrible feeling of doom settled over her, and Slade said nothing as he mounted his horse, his usual cheerful demeanour replaced by an uncharacteristic gloom.

Prunella sighed and stretched her arms behind her. Poor Kelee; Ella couldn't see this going well for her. Authors are so mean to their characters. The poor things suffer so readers can have lots of gripping drama.

Shit, I'm thinking of myself in third person. Let's try it again.

I sigh and stretch my arms behind me, opening my chest. Too much sitting at the computer makes my dancer's body feel tight and cramped. Poor Kelee; I can't see this going well for her. But the dictates of the romance genre require the lovers to be separated— there'd be no plot otherwise. Luckily, it also requires a happy ending. Kelee doesn't know that though, does she?

I write a note for the author and my spell check changes Kelee to Mêlée. Where the hell did Mêlée come from, you stupid computer? What kind of a word is it anyway? Kelee. It's Kelee. Get that into your pro-cessor!

15

Intrusion

My feet pounded the hard earth, jarring my bones, but I couldn't stop. The monster closed in behind me, his breath coming in hard, loud pants. I tripped and stumbled over a fallen branch, only just saving myself from a fall. An evil chuckle reverberated through the darkening forest.

'I'm going to get you, bitch.' The chill in the beast's voice sent shivers down my spine.

I ran faster, my legs burning with the effort, and looked desperately for somewhere to hide, somewhere to escape this monster set on destroying the very fabric of my life. But I knew this forest, and knew there was nowhere here that could keep me safe from this thing bent on revenge.

At least I was making him work for his meal! The thought flashed through my mind, and I smiled— a ray of light in the gloom. My heart lifted. Surely, this couldn't be real. What had I done to turn a man into a monster? Tell him a truth he wasn't willing to hear? Why then had he asked me to tell him?

My breath came in gasps and a stitch formed at my side. I clutched the pain, kept running, and chanced a glance behind. A dark, human-shaped blob wearing a hoodie raced after me, but perhaps he was slowing. I hoped.

The rock! It might be enough. I ran down the track that led to the largest rock in the forest. A tree nestled close behind it. Perhaps I could battle the lantana surrounding it and squeeze between the two. The sticky plant scratched my face and hands and grabbed at my hair as I dived beneath it and crawled to the tree in the middle of the tangle of weeds. Yes! I squeezed myself behind the trunk and, with my back slammed hard against the rock, tried to still my gasping breath. Something crawled over my bare arms. A bite. Ants! I brushed them off and tried not to wriggle, or wonder what else lived in the bark.

The beast crashed through the undergrowth and stopped. I peeked through the scraggly bushes and held my breath. The thing cocked its head and sniffed. God! Could it smell my sweat? The head swivelled and red eyes glowing from beneath the hood fixed on me. An arm pushed back the hood and an evil smile spread slowly over the pale, pockmarked face. Dita?

The monster pulled out a machete—I don't know from where. One minute he had nothing in his hand and the next moment he was attacking the lantana with a machete, cutting a swathe through it towards me. I swallowed in a suddenly dry throat and, sure that something crawled on it, yanked a twig from my long hair.

Wait a minute! I don't have long hair.

My eyes fly open, and I mentally kick myself. I lie warm and safe in my bed, but I've allowed that bullying author to get into my dreamworld. He doesn't belong there. He doesn't belong in any of my worlds! But he's shoved his way in. Despite my determination not to let him get to me, his words have registered somewhere in my psyche, and now, like some virus emerging into its virulent phase, Dita has appeared in my dreams.

Game on!

Next time, I'll have a sword and I'll be able to use it. REALLY WELL.

Report

I stare at the report again, lean back on my office chair and sigh. So it's true. Someone has worked out that, in general, independent authors sell more ebooks and make more money than their mainstream counterparts. Apparently, my author friend Debbie had indeed chosen the right path.

I've tried not to think about the fact that though I sold more books than her in the first month of publication, after that, my sales tailed off while hers kept going. Now she sells more than me, and she earns more from each sale. She didn't have to wait two years to get her book published either. And hers will always be available, not taken off the shelves after less than three months. I had a good team behind me—while it lasted—but she bought her own team, and together they produced a series every bit as good as anything the mainstream produces. The truth I have to face is that, despite the prejudice against self-publishing, it is a viable alternative—if you do it well enough; otherwise it's just embarrassing.

And I've just been dumped by my publisher. They aren't even going to publish one sequel! Debbie published three in the time it took for my one and only book to come out.

Right now, I want to rip my book back off them and republish it myself. They certainly aren't doing anything for it, but I'm pretty sure I signed away the rights for ten years. Ten years! What was I thinking? Oh yeah, I know, I wasn't thinking. I was so proud that someone thought it good enough to publish that I never considered any other option. Debbie has six books out now and is making a name for herself. It's slow, but it's happening. My career is stalling. At least she's in control of her own destiny.

I sigh again and slide my Sequel folder into the archive folder. My on-screen world is not being good to me today.

I feel sick.

I'm far too sensitive.

And I want to live on the other side of the veil.

None of this matters, I tell myself. Suddenly, I feel a strong urge to run away.

17

I am a Goddess

I am a Goddess. I feel like crap. My back aches, my life as a dancer abandoned because of it. One failure. My heart hurts. Love abandoned in its wake. He went to America to continue his career, I remained behind, trying to find my way in the world outside of classes, rehearsals and performances—without the sweat and the buzz. Two failures. Thoughts bewilder my mind. My present career is in tatters and I don't know what to do. Three failures.

I could read all the lovely reviews, but I know that won't sustain me for long. They're just words. Though honestly meant, to my soul they are, in the end, just empty platitudes. So I sit and stare at my shrine and focus on the fact that I am a Goddess.

A Goddess hurting.

I take a deep breath, and as I breathe out, I let it all drop away. Years of practice give me that skill. I place my attention on the pause at the end of my out-breath and remain steadfast there even as I breathe in. The balance shifts and I slip through the gap—a portal to a deeper reality. The world beneath the world

69

emerges; the place where I am invincible, where there is no doubt that my true nature is this glorious Goddess, bejewelled and dressed in silks.

I am such that I can arise as her, or as a thousand different deities, each representing a different aspect of the core of my being; each an interface between the world of form and the world of things yet to manifest. Here, I can affect my reality without mundane struggles. Here, I find peace and clarity and a breadth of vision most people can't even begin to imagine. Here, I have success in every moment, my inner strength and self-worth are unassailable, and this is the only place that really matters, because this is the very ground of existence. All else springs from this.

My legs are in a lotus position, my spine erect. One hand rests on my knee, palm turned out. I hold a flower in the other and sit on a sun and moon-disc seat in the middle of a white lotus. My skin is pure white and I give off a soft white light. I have eyes on the palms of my hands, the soles of my feet and in the centre of my forehead. I am beautiful, and nothing ripples the calm waters of my mind.

I smile and begin the chant. Another deity sits in meditation posture on a lotus in my heart centre, and in the centre of his chest, the syllables of the mantra rotate around a single syllable, the seed of manifestation. Light beams from the top of his head and creates another deity before me, a reflection of me, but clear, as if made of crystal. She smiles, and thousands of replicas of her burst forth and fly to all the corners of the universe, where they collect the vital essence of all existence and draw it back into their mistress. It spirals outward, shining like mercury, from her forehead, throat and heart centre and enters me at the same points. I am filled with this life-affirming nectar.

All is well.

Except that it is difficult for me to accept all the goodness that pours into me. My mind keeps slipping away to mundane things, and I have to keep bringing it back to my meditation. I have to keep returning to this world beneath our world, for habit drags me back to the world of frustration and desire. But even during my mental sabotage—distraction—the constant visualisation and pure sounds of the chant chip away at deeply held feelings of unworthiness. I will practise this for many months until something shifts deep within my being.

Something does shift. Sideways. Into another world.

I am a man—I feel the difference between my legs as I rock slightly with the chant. Maroon robes wrap across my saffron shirt and cover my crossed legs. I sit higher than the other monks, who spread in rows before me in the dim light of a pre-dawn lit only by butter lamps. Incense smoke fills the air and the smell of male bodies hangs thickly in the small space. An ornate shrine with a wealth of images fills the whole of the wall before us. Cloth paintings called tanghkas cover the walls, their images mirroring the true nature of our existence. Deities in their mandalas surround me. I am a deity in the centre of a mandala and so is everyone else here.

This man and this woman, though in different times and spaces, are one, yet not one, different, yet the same, and there is no contradiction. Such is the world beneath the world. His experience enhances mine, and his life informs mine, as mine does his. And neither are inherently what they appear to be. Our true nature is far greater and far freer than most can ever imagine. This world is only open to those who are willing to cast aside their limitations and step beneath the veil.

Thank goodness I have practised long enough to be able to do this; sometimes it's the only thing that keeps me sane.

18

The Yogi

(Somewhere in Tibet before the Chinese invasion.)

My eyes fly open. I cock my head, listening. No sound of movement comes through the door curtain, no bare feet on the pounded-earth floor. No muffled sounds of activity from outside penetrate the thick walls. Even the dogs are silent.

I climb from my bed, open the shutter and peer into the night sky. The light of a full moon washes over me and illuminates my room. Its position dispels any fear that I may have slept too long. The gong that will call the monks to prayer is still some time away. Enough to make my escape.

Today, the saffron robes will remain unworn. The robe of an ordinary man awaits, tucked beneath the blankets so my assistant will not find them. Tashi has done well. The coat he offered just last week fits perfectly and the sturdy boots he provided a month ago in preparation for this day are well worn in now.

I grab my bag—packed the night before—and heft it over my shoulder. Morning practice must wait today. My heart beats with excitement, the like of which

I have never felt before. It quickens often enough with the drums of the dharmapalas' practice and with my morning prostrations, but never like this. My mind is crystal clear, bright and still like the flame on a butter lamp. Alert. Stimulated by the prospect of escape. I shall not miss a moment of this adventure.

I cast a parting glance at the texts neatly stacked in rows along the wall. Others will make use of them now. The main practices I know by heart. I take only a quill, paper and ink.

The curtain parts, and after my passing falls back against the door frame with a swish. My feet propel me through the sleeping monastery. My hand on the wall guides me down the dark corridor. Hesitation doesn't have a chance; the decision was made months ago—months that Tashi has spent preparing for this day. Now it has come, I cannot bear to be here a moment longer.

I open the door slowly, careful not to make a sound, and step outside. A great weight falls from my heart. At last I am free. I close the door softly behind me and take a deep breath of the chilly air. No incense smoke here, no smell of a hundred men and boys packed together. Even the smells of the village are muted by the cold. Guided by the moonlight, I hurry off and don't look back.

After only a few steps, an unexpected mix of emotions arise. I watch them with curiosity until they fade in the vast expanse of my mind. I had expected the relief, but not the grief. But I suppose it is not surprising. The monastery has been my home since my parents brought me here in my fourth year. I have been blessed with excellent spiritual instruction from great masters—I mentally prostrate to my root master—but the administration, the hierarchy, the responsibilities, even the set practices have become impediments rather than the support they once were. Though my mind is free wherever I am, it is time for this body to part ways with the monastery that nurtured it. There are advanced practices on which I need to focus, and for which only solitude will suffice. I wince at the possibility that this is a great delusion, a trap set by my ego, but my heart, where the mind of my master resides, says, 'go'.

'You have all the teachings, now go and practise them,' he had said.

My time as a monk is over. The life of a yogi awaits me.

I run my hand over my skull and feel the stubble. Today is shaving day, but this head will not see a razor or scissors again. A laugh escapes my lips. None of that matters where I am going. Tashi will have a hat to keep my head warm until I have hair long enough to wrap around it.

I arrive at my first destination and tap on the door of Tashi's house. A light shines through the cracks in the shutters. I hope he got some sleep. The door opens, and I am greeted by a broad smile. He bows. I bow in return, and he gestures me inside. His bedroll lies on the floor by the door where he waited for my knock.

'All is ready, your—'

With a hand gesture, I cut him off before he can speak my title. He nods. We have spoken about this. I do not want to be anybody any more, just an anonymous yogi living alone in the mountains. Perhaps one day I will return, but for now, I go incognito.

I refuse tea. We can stop later and make some on the way. I wish to be far from the village by the time everyone wakes. They will not find a note on my bed. They will know from the robes I left behind that the time has come for this lama to relinquish his seat. They know that Tashi, like his father before him, is my benefactor, and they will find out when he returns.

'I will have to tell them eventually,' he says, handing me a fleece-lined hat, 'but I will keep them at bay as long as I can.'

I pull the hat down over my ears and open the door. 'If they come to visit, I shall throw stones at them until they go away,' I say as I step outside.

The I who writes this is not the I who lived it, and yet I feel the ache in his legs as he climbs. I smile with him when he reaches his new home and gazes at the vastness of the view with the monastery and village just a speck in the distance. I feel his gratitude when he sees how comfortable Tashi has made the cave; it must have taken him many trips—half a day each—to make it habitable again. The man's devotion cannot be questioned.

Is this a past life creeping into my present awareness or is it simply a product of a writer's imagination? It could be either and is likely the latter, for I live the lives of all my characters to some extent.

Either way, I know what this monk does not know on this day, and I see what he cannot see at this time. He will stay on this mountain longer than three years, three months and three days, and he will watch helplessly as his monastery burns.

19

Phone Call

Though it's taking far too long, I'm enjoying editing Kelee's World. The scene laid out on my computer screen is in Kelee's bedroom in the Menhir Mansion. The way the author describes the house makes me think of the old buildings in the south of France— terracotta tiled roofs, thick granite walls, small windows, polished floorboards and heavy rugs. Kelee's bed is a lush four-poster complete with drapery—as you'd expect in a period romance—and I expect that the room is fairly dim. I focus on the words:

Someone rapped on the door, the thick wood ringing beneath their knuckles.

'Who is it?' Kelee called from where she lay on her bed reading the heavy tome Miramar had left her.

''Tis Suzie, Miss.'

'Come in, then.'

The door opened and the servant girl took a timid step into the room before bobbing her white-capped head in deference. 'Your mother calls for you. Master Beak is here. He wishes to see you.'

Kelee grimaced. 'I don't wish to see him.'

A grin transformed Suzie's plain face as if lit from within. 'She said you'd say that, and she said she wants you to come down anyway.'

'And do what? Have a cup of coffee and a polite chat?'

Suzie giggled and shoved a wayward brown curl back under her cap.

'Is that so funny?'

She nodded. 'I can't imagine you ever being polite to Master Beak, not really.'

'He's a creep; you can see that, can't you?'

'Of course, Miss. Everyone can see that.'

'Except my mother.'

Suzie shrugged. 'He'll have a big inheritance coming his way when his father dies, and that's not so long away. There's plenty would have him for that alone.'

'But not me.'

'No, Miss, not you. Will you humour your mother and come down, though?'

Kelee slammed the book shut, shoved it beneath her pillow and swung her legs off the side of the bed. 'Indeed, since she's not well, but only to make it very clear to Master Beak that I want nothing to do with him.'

The phone rings. I jump. Damn telemarketers. I pick up the receiver.

'Hello, this is Ella.' I wait for the silence that marks a call coming from a call centre in Asia or India,

the pause that's my signal to hang up before someone
begins their spiel.

'Hi, Ella. It's Scott.'

'Scott? … Oh! … Scott.' The guy from the
party. Heat flushes my face. I'd almost forgotten about
him. 'I was focusing on a manuscript. Off with the
pixies.' And I never actually thought he would ring.

'I was wondering if you'd like to go to dinner
sometime.'

'Ooh, a date, that's different.' I grimace. What a
stupid thing to say. Not that I care, actually. I gave up
thoughts of romance when I moved into my inheritance here in the bush.

'You mean you don't have men lined up at your
door?' His voice is nice—smooth and deep.

I chuckle. 'I think the locals are all taken.'

'Not this one.' I can hear the twinkle in his eye,
see the little smile lines.

'I thought you were only staying a couple of
weeks.'

'I was, but the person I'm looking for is proving
hard to find.'

'Who is it? I might know them.' Unlikely, but it
seemed polite to ask.

'Just some vindictive old biddy who's been
causing a bit of a problem for me, but I really don't
want to talk about it.'

'Fair enough.'

When he speaks again, there's vulnerability in his tone. 'Will you come? I'd very much like your company.'

I hesitate. I can't really afford the time right now. I'm not going to be able to have a weekend until this editing is done, but … 'Of course, I'll come. I'd love to.' Liz would kill me if I turned him down, and it might be nice—he might be nice. Besides, it's a free dinner and probably better than what I can cook.

'Excellent.'

We set a time and a place, and end the call. The conversation, short though it was, leaves me with a warm feeling. Perhaps it isn't too late. A husband and kids weren't on my agenda when I danced, and we never had time for much socialising outside of the company anyway. Some formed liaisons within the tribe, and I had the usual affairs—we were a promiscuous bunch—but only Tom ever felt like Mr Right. And he showed me how wrong I was about that.

After that, I spent three years in Buddhist Retreat at a Tibetan temple in the south of France—not the best place for finding a man—and I spent most of my degree travelling back and forth from here, so no socialising there. If Scott really is as good as he seems, then the universe is definitely looking out for me. But I'm not about to get my hopes up. I don't mind this journey remaining solo.

Kelee, however, is turning suitors away, but she's eighteen and lives in a village, and being the protagonist of a romance, she is also gorgeous—white skin, tall and slender with a curvy body and long black hair. Beside her, I'm ancient and tiny. No boobs to speak of and I cut my hair short for my farewell party from the company. Before that, I'd been a picture perfect ballerina, short and light—easy to lift—with big eyes, though boring grey, and an aristocratic nose.

I turn my attention back to my work and grin as I watch Kelee attack Beak with finely honed sarcasm. He has no idea what's going on, and Kelee's mum, bless her, just purses her lips and smiles.

20

Reciprocal Lies

I stare at my computer screen in disbelief. What has happened to my 'Like' numbers? I'm sure I had more than that. I did have more than that! Around twenty people have unliked my Facebook page.

It stinks of Dita. Has he contacted them all and told them lies about me? Bribed them, even? How low would he stoop?

It hurts. I hate to say it, but it does. Those Likes are hard won. They represent the results of hours of marketing efforts, and it disgusts me that twenty is a big number to lose. If I had thousands it wouldn't matter. Right now, I wish I wasn't an author. The whole thing sucks.

I run my hand through my hair and sigh. It hangs limp against my head today, but that's not why I sigh. There's nothing I can do about the lost Likes. Not a single thing.

I remind myself they're not real, only an arrangement of pixels on a screen. A number cannot harm me—unless I let it.

And I will not let it.

I will remain on the top of my metaphorical mountain, my mind elevated above this worldly nonsense.

The notifications mentioned a message, which is why I'm on my Facebook page. I click to read it.

'Hi, I write awesome fantasy. I just liked your page, please like mine back.'

I grit my teeth and actually growl in frustration. I may have just lost twenty likes, but I am not, and will never be, that desperate.

Like my page and I'll like yours. Ugh! What if I actually don't like yours, or I haven't read your book so I don't know whether I like it or not? Like something as an exchange deal and you might just be declaring to the world that you like crap.

I feel a blog post coming on, so I open a new document and start typing.

Swapping Likes isn't honest and it isn't ethical, and it isn't even how karma works. Why? Because karma works on intention. You might be able to fool a person about your motivations, but you can't fool karma. Self-serving actions create negative karma, and negative karma is not good for you. One day it will come back and bite your butt. In fact, it's nibbling right now; you just don't know it.

Numbers might look impressive, but what's more important is how many of those people actually care a hoot about you or what you do. You don't get that with a Like-swap.

Like-swap. I smile at the neologism. And I feel better now. I've just reminded myself that those twenty Likes don't equal book sales. But the topic of ethics in the new world of 'anything goes' publishing raises another issue I don't intend to leave out of the post.

As for swapping five star reviews? Suggest that to me and you won't get a review, you'll get a lecture on ethics and the value of honest feedback. Yeah, I do that kind of thing. Swapping five star reviews makes a mockery of the whole review system and treats readers like gullible idiots. Totally not cool. No way. Don't even think about it.

Rants make good blog posts.

The topic leaves me cold, though. It's why I sometimes wish I wasn't an author. Some would say my ethics are naive and that since everyone does it, it's okay. But since when did the number of people doing something make it right?

21

The Date

Clothes I never wear fill my too-small wardrobe, but hiding somewhere amongst the squash must be the perfect outfit. Surely. I flip through the garments; snippets of memories fly like moths from each one, and some even form tentative story threads. The black suit I wore to my mother's funeral hangs beside a short, glittering sheath, a remnant from my clubbing days. My soft Indian pants trail the ground next to my favourite gypsy skirt. That might work, and I haven't worn it for ages. I snort. All I wear these days is trackies and microfiber T-shirts and jumpers to keep me warm. Even when I look for something classy to wear to town, this wardrobe stays closed. I really do need to throw some of these out, most of them actually. I only keep them for days like this, for the rare times I need to look ... what? Elegant, classy, sexy, cultured? How do I want to appear to Scott tonight?

If I don't hurry up, I'm going to be late. I spent way too much time editing, but I needed to get the day's quota out of the way.

I sigh, leave the wardrobe door agape and flop back onto my bed. I didn't spend three years of formal spiritual practice, scriptural study and listening to teachings given by eminent masters just to come back here and angst over what to wear on a date. I'm past playing games. But I enjoy good food, and I can't go to a fancy restaurant in trackies, so the question of what to wear must be answered. I check my watch. Now.

Dresses say you're trying; skirts say you're not trying but still want to be feminine; pants are comfortable and what I wear mostly anyway, except on hot summer days, so pants it is. I grab a black pair and a classy aqua top and pull them on. They'll do. I am not going to angst over this date.

A vague hope festers inside me. I laugh at it and it fades, taking its partner fear with it. I'm completely fine being alone. I'm never lonely, and I have Merlin to talk to. My life is one of silence and the written word. Perhaps that's strange, but it's my life, and I like it. I blast my awareness onto the wondering about a future with Scott that creeps into my consciousness and watch the projections shatter into a million harmless pieces then fade away. Traps, all of them. Mental freedom is my most cherished possession. I will not be trapped by what-ifs.

Make-up? The answer is easy: no. He'll have me as I am, or not at all. My only deference to how my head looks is a brush through my hair, after which I spike it up so the shape is right. I'm at the bedroom door when I sigh and return to the mirror. I add some eye shadow and liner and a touch of lippy. He might be insulted if I don't look like I've made a little effort.

Then I drive to the restaurant. I wouldn't expect, and didn't want, anyone to drive all the way up here to get me.

***

The lights of the harbour sparkle on the gentle swell of the waves. The fishing boats in the little marina bob up and down, and a couple cuddle on a foreshore bench.

'Ella?'

'Huh?' I drag my gaze back through the restaurant window and look at the man before me— one of the most self-absorbed people I've ever met. His mouth moves like that of a fish out of water—blurble blurble—and I no longer hear his words. The subtle rising of a hope for a future with him turned into boredom about half an hour after he started talking. A total info dump—all about him and how rich and successful he is. My impression of him is one of blandness and insecurity trying to impress with name-dropping and stories of glittering parties. I remember him saying he was in real estate but that's about all.

He frowns; his eyes have a desperate shine to them now. 'What about you?'

He must have got my unsubtle message. Truly, I had zoned out. I had tried to be interested. It just felt like a kind of sales pitch. 'Ex ballet dancer. That pretty much sums it up. When my mum died, I came here and set up an editing business.'

'You're an editor? Wow, that's amazing; I—um. You must know all the authors around here, then.'

'No. My clients are all overseas. If there are any authors around here, I've not met them.' I didn't mention my own status in that area; right now, my already battered writer self didn't want to hear yet another person say they hadn't heard of my book.

Scott opens his mouth as if to say something, then apparently changes his mind and closes it again. He stares out the window with a frown, as if struggling over something. The silence becomes a little uncomfortable.

I scan the restaurant, wondering if it's too early to terminate the date. Other couples sit in quiet conversation punctuated by the clatter of cutlery. I wonder if they've messed up the white linen table cloths like I have. Wait staff in black move efficiently between the tables, their skin burnished by the soft lights. How many of those bright smiles mask tiredness and boredom like mine does?

I turn back to him. 'It's been lovely, Scott, but I need to go. I have a lot of work to do tomorrow and I want to get a good day in.'

His handsome face crumples in disappointment. 'Don't you want dessert?'

I only just stop myself from automatically saying, 'Some other time.' There won't be another time. I know why his marriage broke up, and it wasn't the reason he'd told me. I shake my head. 'I'm sorry. I really am.' And I am. I would have liked him to be different.

I stand.

He stands with me. 'How about we go dancing?' he asks. I frown, and he adds quickly, 'Just as friends. We can get dressed to the nines, drink far too much and giggle like schoolgirls. It'll be fun.'

I press my lips together. Drinking too much had never been my idea of fun. I have too much respect for my body.

'What's the matter?' A slight bitterness creeps into his tone. 'Don't you like dressing sexy?'

I roll my eyes. He has no idea. The man is way out of his zone. He just doesn't know it. They didn't use to call me Sexie Lexie for nothing.

22

Memory of a Pseudonym

Electra stared across the parking lot. The distance between the car and the door of the pub was just a little too far should anyone follow her out. Damn. Usually she found a park closer, but there was a big crowd today. And damn again that she had to park out the front and walk the gamut of the public bar to get to the dressing room. Why they couldn't let them go in the back way was beyond her. No, actually, she got it. Girls in glamorous make up striding through the bar whetted the men's appetite, made them buy another drink because it wouldn't be long before the girls came on.

She sighed and grabbed her bag from the passenger seat. At least she didn't have to work up the Cross. She didn't have to do this kind of work at all, did she? Actually, you do, she reminded herself. Without the stripping, she'd have to find a job working on the other side of the bar, or in an office. Yikes. What a waste of all those years of training. Some would say that this was a waste as well. Nah! She loved every bit of it.

Except walking across the parking lot and through the bar.

She left the car, locked it and walked across the exposed gravel, her runners crunching with each step. The sounds of glasses clunking on tables and men talking and laughing too loudly wafted through the open door. Blobs with thick necks and sun-browned heads moved around on the other side of the grimy windows, and cracks spread from a central point across the old green tiles on the outer walls—the remands of some heavy impact.

The stripper grinned. She'd be making an impact today.

A truck roared past on the road behind her, and she strode into the bar.

The sound level dropped. Heads turned; eyes raked her body—sizing up her tits. Her tattered jeans and baggy sweater didn't fool anyone, not as long as she wore the glam make-up and lush wig. She fixed her eyes on the door at the other end of the bar and sauntered through the gloom as if her heart wasn't kicking just a little too hard in her chest. The talking resumed. She figured that some of it referred to her now.

'Hey, gorgeous; ya got a kiss for Mikey here?' Someone called from the other side of the room. A barrage of chuckles followed.

'You wish,' she shot back, and the chuckling ratcheted up a notch.

Bob, the owner, nodded at her from behind the bar where he polished glasses with chubby fingers— nice bloke, Bob; big, flabby and no oil painting, but decent. The old guys hanging round the pool table tipped imaginary hats at her, and the group at the table at the end of the bar gave her smiles of encouragement. They had kind eyes. She recognised Pete and smiled back.

She danced for good blokes like him and his mates. To bring some beauty and glamour into their hardworking concrete suburbia lives. Most of these men went home to their wife and children after the five-thirty show.

The Creep made his move just before she got to the door marked Private. He slipped out of the shadows and stepped between her and the door as if he'd been waiting for just that moment. She recoiled at his sudden appearance.

He placed his hand on the door and pushed. 'After you, Miss Electra,' he said with feigned politeness and a twisted smile. The door swung open, but he didn't move aside to let her pass. His hard eyes glittered in the light of the exit sign. He fixed them on her, and his smile turned into a sneer.

Though her heart jumped a beat or two, she held his gaze without flinching. The guy got off on fear—she felt that in her bones—and she would not give him the satisfaction. 'Thanks,' she said. For nothing, Creep.

'Leave the lady alone, mate.' Pete suddenly appeared beside her, arms flexed, muscles straining against his work-soiled T-shirt. He stood a good head taller than her, and though his sandy beach-boy hair looked sweet and innocent next to The Creep's dark, greasy locks, he had good reason to be proud of his body. No one in his right mind would mess with Pete. He'd proved that when he'd hauled The Creep off her last time she worked here.

'I's jus opening the door for 'er.' The Creep stepped back. His arm no longer held the door open and it swung closed in front of her.

Electra pushed past him, shoved open the door and slipped through, casting a smile of gratitude back over her shoulder at Pete before the door swung shut behind her. The Creep wouldn't have come in with her anyway. Bob would bar him from the pub for that, and that would be after Pete used his muscle to explain why he shouldn't mess with the girls. Electra smiled. Pete had told her last time that he'd be happy to walk her to her car anytime. All she had to do was ask. But something in her resisted asking for help.

She walked beneath a dusty, naked bulb along a corridor with scratched green-tinged walls lined with boxes of glasses, past the empty kitchen and the staff toilet, and opened the door into a storeroom that once a week doubled as a dressing room.

Saucy Sal was already there, lounging on a plastic chair and dragging on a joint. Her full breasts, half obscured beneath a lacy white shirt, strained against a tiny sequin bra, and a stomach that had seen better days rolled slightly over a bright green and very mini mini-skirt. Her long legs, topped with lethal heels, stretched towards a dusty single bar radiator. She looked up and smiled. The make-up around her eyes cracked slightly.

'Wanna toke?' She held out the joint.

Electra nodded, took the joint and sucked in a lungful. 'Thanks.' She'd had some before she left home, but a top-up was always welcome.

'I had to beg for the heater,' Sal croaked in a thick Sydney accent.

Electra released a swathe of smoke and handed back the joint. 'Glad you did. It'd be freezing in here otherwise.' She dumped her bag on the other chair and laid out her first costume. Two girls, two shows each. Twelve minutes a pop. One hundred and fifty dollars a gig, and she got to dance. There were worse ways to earn a living.

'I'm done with that,' Sal said, jerking her head to the mirror that sat propped against the wall on the plastic fold-out table. She patted her bottle-blonde hair. 'Can't turn this old sow into silk anymore.'

'Go on, you look great.' Considering she was pushing forty and had smoked all her life.

'Aw, you're a sweet kid, Lexie. I like working with you.' She offered the joint again. There wasn't much left.

'Likewise.' Electra took the joint, took a couple of tokes and offered it back.

Sal waved her away. 'Finish it.'

Lexie did, then she stripped down to a tiny G-string, then added layers of black lace and leather over the top so she could take them off again to music in front of a room full of men. The stripper chuckled at the absurdity of it. Once all dolled up in her silver chains, black leathers and studs, she perched on the edge of the chair and dragged on her high stiletto boots.

'Sweet and tough,' Sal mused as Lexie stared into the too small mirror and used a brush to add a layer of rich red to her lips. 'I'm sweet and frilly, and you're the bad ass in the leather jacket. They get the best of both worlds.'

Lexie nodded. Sal was old school. She didn't so much dance as wiggle and writhe, and much of her show made a good anatomy lesson for anyone interested in the bits that usually stay covered. Lexie, on the other hand, was the new breed of stripper. She danced—sometimes hard and fast, sometimes soft and sexy. What Lexie lacked in tits, she made up for in looks and talent. Ex-ballet dancers make awesome strippers. The blokes loved them both. And the girls respected each other's acts no matter what they were. The sheer diversity of self-expression was one of the things that made the circuit popular, and—for Lexie at least—interesting.

Lexie surreptitiously checked that she'd pinned her wig on well enough. The long, red-brown hair was a tad too close to the ballet dancer she'd been until a year ago, but take it off and no one would recognise the girl with the short blonde spikes that hid underneath.

'Getting much work?' Sal asked.

'Enough.' Lexie wrapped her fake hair into a roll and tucked it under her German airman's cap, a genuine relic from World War Two. 'You?'

'Not as much as I used to.'

Lexie glanced at the woman she knew as Sal and wondered what her real name was. Maybe it was Sally; who knew? Lexie had never told any of the other girls her real name—obviously, it wasn't Electra, but it wasn't Lexie either—and she certainly wouldn't ask anyone else their real name. What did it matter, anyway? Despite the fact that Sal looked like she needed a friend right now, Lexie wasn't going to hang out with her when they weren't working.

A knock sounded on the door. 'You girls decent?'

'Yep,' Sal yelled, then coughed and giggled at the same time.

Bob poked his head in the door. 'Music.'

Lexie grabbed her CDs from where she'd laid them on the table and handed them over.

Bob waited while Sal ferreted in the mess at the bottom of her bag.

'Okay, Miss Electra, let's go,' Bob said, once he had four CDs in his hand. 'You're on.'

Lexie grabbed her riding crop and followed him out.

'Break a leg,' Sal called after her.

Ballet or stripping, it made little difference.

23

Carl and Clarrisa

Sometimes I think my creative mind is a curse. Here I am, sitting peacefully, supposed to be meditating, and I'm talking to Carl and Clarissa instead—they're the characters from my book *Catnip Creek*. Actually, it's possibly their fault, if it's a fault at all. They have taken the opportunity to make contact while my mind is in that lovely clear, vibrant space beneath the veil.

It's the world of creativity, brimming with un-manifested possibilities, some of which will manifest, most of which won't. Perhaps some people create from their ordinary mind, but not me. Here, unlimited worlds stretch endlessly in all directions, and when my mind is open, creativity rushes in like water into an open drain.

I'm never sure whether to ignore it and continue my meditation or write it down before the vivid reality of the scenes dissolves and cannot be re-called. I usually write them down. The meditative state remains through the writing, anyway, so I'm not really stopping meditating, just acting while in meditation. At least that's how I rationalise it. Perhaps, I'm fooling myself, or perhaps it's what they call divine inspiration—it feels like it could be that—but the terminology doesn't matter. I'm not actually distracted from that deep state of awareness, just dipping into the realm of plenitude, what Buddhists call the Sambhogakaya.

'You think too much,' Clarissa says.

'And it's rude to go into an internal monologue while someone is talking to you,' Carl said. He's not angry though. His eyes twinkle, animating the laugh lines around his eyes and mouth. He cocks his head and fixes his steel grey eyes on me. I smile at the familiar grin. He's like an old friend. 'I am an old friend,' he says. 'And I'm telepathic with you, so don't forget it.'

Clarissa plonks her fists on her ample hips and purses her lips. Strands of white hair escape from her bun and shine in the sunlight. Her eyebrows curve high above her pretty blue eyes, reminding me of her question. The water gurgles happily in Catnip Creek behind her. 'Well?'

I sigh and survey the lush veggie garden, lovingly tended by this adorable couple. Their cat, Hubert, suns himself on the stone bench, his black fur in stark contrast to the bleached stone. Carl's earth-brown britches—his word, not mine—are filthy from working in the garden. He likes to get down into it, as he says.

'I do. Now, answer the question!' He rubs his hand across his bald head. His arm muscles strain against his old blue shirt, sleeves rolled to the elbow.

'Yep, get on with it.' Clarissa, of course. They're a formidable team.

'The publisher isn't interested.' Disappointment fills my words. I can't help it. But I see it for what it is, just a cloud passing across the sky of my mind. It hangs around for a while, but it doesn't touch the pure blue above it.

'Oh dear, I am so sorry.' Without hesitation, Clarissa crosses the few steps between us and gives me a hug as generous as her bosom and as strong as her determination. I smile and mumble my thanks. She pats my back.

Carl harrumphs, grips his hoe tighter and plants his feet more firmly on the ground. 'And you're going to let that stop you, are you?'

I disengage from the hug. 'Why bother when hardly anyone read the first one? I do actually need to earn a living, you know. And the time spent writing your story could be spent earning a dollar.'

Clarissa nods. 'Of course, dear, we understand.' She turns to her husband with her agree-with-me-or-else look. 'Don't we, Carl?'

He frowns. 'But it's such a good story.'

I wave my arm to the sky. 'The minds of humans are full of good stories, but that doesn't mean we have to write every one of them down.'

'Are you saying our story isn't good enough?' He folds his arms across his chest and rocks backwards and forwards from his heels to the balls of his feet.

'Carl!' Clarissa's sharp tone makes me wince. 'That isn't the point. The point is that she doesn't have funds to live on, and the book is unlikely to give her decent returns on her time. Would you plant a crop under those conditions, no matter how delicious it was?'

Carl grimaces. 'Fine, I get it. I just think your world could do with a bit more love and light in the way they deal with their problems. People could learn from our story.'

'I know, that's why I wrote the first one, but people will only learn if they actually read the book.' The couple nod with sad resignation. Hubert stretches and yawns. 'I'm really sorry,' I say, my heart aching.

Clarissa sighs, and in the following silence, the cat jumps off the bench, saunters along the path and rubs himself against my legs.

'Our story will always be here,' Carl says. 'We lived it and stamped it in time. And even though we will move on, you'll always be able to re-enter the time of the challenge and write it for your world should you wish.'

Clarissa smiles again, and I can't help but smile back. The scene fades, but the sun still feels warm against my skin and a cat rubs against my legs. I look down. Merlin, not Hubert, bunts me and looks up with expectant eyes.

'What do you want, kitten?'

Duh! A game, stupid human.

'No time for games now,' I tell him. 'I have to get to work.'

24

Kelee's World

Kelee sat at her dressing table and smiled at herself in the mirror.

Her maid stood behind her, grinning at a job well done. She'd spent a good hour helping her mistress into her gown and fussing over her hair and make-up. 'Perfect.' She brushed her hands against each other. 'You'll have all the young men swooning at your feet.'

Kelee didn't want them all at her feet. She wanted Slade at her side. But Miranda was right, they may not swoon exactly, but they'd be vying for a spot on her dance card. She had to admit that the girl who stared back at her from the mirror was the epitome of Magan beauty; thick black hair—partly piled on her head and wreathed in a gold and emerald circlet for the ball—high cheekbones, red lips and brilliant green eyes on pale skin. All of that and the chief's daughter as well—heiress to coffers full of gold—would have them swarming like flies around a carcass.

She stood and spun before the mirror. The light from the oil lamps sparkled off the gemstones on her fitted scarlet bodice and shimmered across the taffeta skirt that spread generously from a low waistline in a riot of tucks and flounces. Her grandmother's emerald necklace wreathed her neck in delicate swirls, matching her eyes perfectly.

'Come, come, you should be there already,' the maid said, holding a white lace shawl ready to slip around her charge's shoulders.

Kelee brushed a perfectly curled strand of hair off her face, accepted the shawl and left the room with the white-capped maid trotting at her heels.

They stopped at the end of the corridor at the top of the stairs. Kelee peeked around the corner and through the banisters to the crowd below. Where was Slade? He should be here by now. She'd provided the invitation and the clothes. She smiled as she remembered how fine he'd looked in her brother's old formal gear.

Had he chickened out? No. Slade had all the education he needed to be comfortable at the ball. His mother had been born into a noble family; she'd just married a poor man, but she'd taught her children everything they needed to know to move up in the world. And though he didn't care where in society his place happened to be, Slade had looked forward to the ball. He'd treated it as an adventure, and his mother had been thrilled. Besides, they both knew that if her parents saw how well he fitted into society they just might allow a marriage. But he wasn't here. And she'd told him to wait at the bottom of the stairs.

'Go on, Miss,' the maid urged.

Kelee recognised Beak and clenched her teeth. He waited at the bottom of the stairs, without a doubt waiting for her. She turned back.

'Miss, where are you going?'

'I'll use the back stairs.'

The maid grabbed her arm. 'You can't, Miss, they're all expecting you to make an entrance.'

Kelee sighed. Her father would be furious if he couldn't display his daughter as he wished. Maid was right; she would just have to bear it.

'Go on. You'll be fine. They'll all love you.' The maid pressed her hand into the small of Kelee's back.

Kelee nodded. 'Sure. I'll see you later.'

When she appeared at the top of the curved staircase, all eyes in the foyer turned to her and tracked her progress downward. An awed silence fell, and even those in the ballroom turned and stared through the double doors. Her father, in his starched white shirt and black trousers, strode towards her with gleaming eyes, wearing his pride for all to see, and her mother glided after him. Her brother Kestril stood on the opposite side of the stairs to Beak, and he gave a rare smile, his eyes twinkling with the warmth he reserved for her.

Her heart pounded with nerves, praying that her father would take her hand instead of Beak, but as she reached the last few steps, Beak stepped forward and her father stopped. Just when she thought Beak would claim her, Kestril took the two steps up to meet her and lifted his elbow, inviting her to thread her arm through his. His smile deepened, and his green eyes, fixed on hers, told her that he knew she'd needed rescuing.

She accepted his offer. 'Thank you,' she whispered as they took the last few steps side by side.

He nodded. 'My pleasure. And you are far too young to be claimed yet by any man.'

'Especially that one.' She indicated Beak with her eyes.

Kestril nodded. 'Especially that one.'

Annoyance rolled off Beak in waves as they walked past him without any indication of having seen him. Her father stepped before them, brought his heels together and gave a little bow to his son, and then to his daughter. 'What a fine pair you make,' he said, 'but I hope you will not keep her long, Kestril.'

'Of course not, Father,' he replied, 'but she should not be claimed by only one of these many fine young men drooling for her company.'

'I totally agree,' their mother added as she joined them.

'Yes, of course.'

Kelee smiled. Her father knew when he'd been outwitted. Though a tough leader of the clan, he was a reasonable father.

'I trust you have a card to ensure that you give all your prospective beaus a fair chance.'

Kelee's mother tossed her elegant head, making her dark brown waves dance around the sharply defined features of her face. 'Of course, she does.'

Kelee patted the little pocket on the hip of her gown. A dance card and tiny pencil nestled inside.

Her father stepped away, creating a gap for Beak to step into, but Kestril pulled Kelee towards the ballroom before their cousin had a chance to make his move. 'Her first dance will be with me,' he said, 'unless she objects, of course. I want to see if she has learnt her lessons better than last time.'

Kelee laughed. 'No objections, Brother. Let's go.' She felt Beak seething behind them as they strode to the dance floor and was doubly grateful for the unexpected ally. Her brother's perceptiveness constantly surprised her.

'He can take his turn like everyone else,' Kestril said.

'Have you seen Slade?' she whispered.

He turned to her, one eyebrow raised in query.

'I gave him your old formal clothes. I hope you don't mind.'

'Not at all. But I have not seen him here, either in or out of my old clothes. I trust he knows how to dance.'

Kelee rolled her eyes. 'His mother is a Beech.'

'Ah, yes, of course. Noble blood runs in his veins. But even without it, dear Sister, he is still more worthy of you than that scoundrel Beak.'

'You'll talk to Father?'

'I will.' He patted her arm.

Neither brother nor sister saw the stable boy as they twirled around the dance floor, and though after dancing with her brother, Kelee wandered the room, trying to escape Beak and look as if she wasn't searching for someone, Slade never showed.

25

Exploding Email

I check the time, lean back in my office chair, raise my arms above my head and arch my back in a luxurious stretch. It's time for a break. Kelee's story takes an intense focus, and I have a lot of work to do, but I can't keep that level of concentration up indefinitely.

Besides, the sun is shining and the pond is full. My anticipation is so strong that I already feel the water caressing my skin. But I should check my emails first. I'm hoping the author with the big editing job has decided to pay my bills for the next month.

I click on the browser icon and stand while it's loading. A few plies keep my legs alive, and Merlin takes the opportunity to amble up and ask for a game by forcefully bunting my leg. Maybe, I'll tie him up outside while I have a swim.

The computer screen is like a window into another world, into countless worlds. Every webpage is someone's world, and every article is someone's story. Even the Gmail inbox appearing on the screen is a kind of a world. It's like a landing pad out of, or an entrance way into, the worlds of the senders.

My heart skips a beat—again—and that annoys the crap out of me. It's an email for God's sake, not a loaded gun! Or maybe it is. Dita's name—in bold—has just blown my morning. That and the subject line: Notification of Legal Action. What world exactly does this man live in?

I should delete it unopened. I know I should. My cursor hovers over the garbage bin, but my curiosity gets the better of me; the subject line is too intriguing. I grit my teeth and open it. No one can be sued for a review, can they?

I check my mind and make sure it's calm before I read. I'll not let him mess up my equanimity this time.

After careful evaluation of the events leading up to the posting of your review, I have decided that I had no choice but to seek legal counsel. My attorney has assured me with 100% certainty that I not only have a case for slander and libel, but that you yourself might be working with other authors in an attempt to discredit me and my work. My lawyer has also assured me that with the evidence that I have collected from your review, your website and our correspondence that you will likely face the maximum penalty - in a case like this that will equate to roughly $150,000 in damages and up to 18 months of prison time.

I would like to avoid this scenario as much as you, so I will again give you the opportunity to take down the offending review within 24 hours. This time, failure to comply will result in a lawsuit being swiftly filed with the California grand court and a cease-and-desist order will be issued against you and any other aliases you may use on the Internet. My attorney has assured me that not only will we have your Internet abilities re-voked almost instantly, but that we can file an injunction to keep you from filing for bankruptcy and avoiding the cost of your criminal activity.

Again, I implore you to simply take down the review. I think we can both agree that this isn't worth going to court over, and I would hate to have to ruin someone's life over something as silly as a poorly-written and misguided review. I hope to hear back from you soon with acknowledgement of this letter and assurance that the review will be taken down in the allotted time. If not, the next letter you get will definitely be from my legal team.

I shake my head, not knowing quite what to make of it. Does he really believe this will scare me? That it will make me run, quaking, to my computer desperate to take the review down before I end up in a Californian jail charged with writing a defamatory review?

I giggle at the absurdity of it. $150,000! I'm pretty sure it would get laughed out of any court in the Western world. If anyone can see anything libellous in my carefully worded review then they're wearing the same strange glasses as Dita, and his vision is badly impaired by anger, insecurity and disappointment. I do truly feel for Dita, but his book still stinks. He should be grateful I didn't actually use those words.

I could be wrong, of course; there might just be one court somewhere willing to set a precedent so that no author will ever have to put up with a bad review ever again.

The whole scenario is too bizarre to cause me much upset, but I do wonder at how far he might be willing to go in his vendetta, and that gives me reason to pause. Anxiety sets my cells aquiver until I make a conscious effort to calm myself.

I'll not be bullied into taking the review down, and I'll deal with whatever happens when it happens. I'll not cause myself trauma by imagining things that may never happen—like not meeting the deadline!

Thoughts of how unfair it is, of how I don't deserve it, of how someone should be able to stop it and of how I will not bow to his pressure assail my mind and override what it should be thinking about—work. Once again, I have no choice, I either let the mental torment continue or I take control of my mind and rip the cycle of thoughts out at their root. I go for the ripping.

26

Another Call

Tring tring; tring tring!

I flinch. The telephone rings rarely here, and the harsh sound shatters the still morning. Who rings at nine in the morning anyway? I plonk my elbow on my desk and reach for the receiver.

'Hello.' I don't even try to sound enthusiastic. I'm about to start work, and I expect it'll be a junk call.

'Ella?' A man's voice.

'Yes, who's this?' I stare out the window into the sunshine and note that the veggie patch needs weeding.

'Scott. Hi.'

'Oh. Hi.' My heart drops and my voice turns from suspicious to flat.

'I was wondering if you'd like to go dancing with me in Wollongong.' He sounds … sad … as if he expects me to say no.

'Umm.' I'm wondering how to get out of this as quickly and kindly as possible.

'Just as a friend, of course,' he adds quickly.

'Of course. Trouble is, I am really busy at the moment.' I scan my desk—computer on, sticky notes in place, mouse at the ready, cat napping, all ready to go.

'You work Saturday nights?' he asks with more than a little disbelief.

I gulped. No; I watch movies. 'When I have to. I've got a big job on, the author wants it done by a set date and I'm really not sure I'll make it.'

'Oh. I see. I …' His voice is barely over a whisper. 'Is delivering late really a problem?'

'She can ask for her advance back—and this woman would. She's desperate to get the book out.'

'Oh. Maybe … no … I mean … it's not healthy to work all the time. You should get out more.'

Huh! Like he knows me so well! 'I get out enough. And, frankly, nightclubs don't really do it for me these days. Besides, I really can't afford the time.'

'Oh, come on, live a little.'

I winced at the cliché, and the whine in his voice totally killed any chance he might have had of convincing me. 'I think your view of what constitutes living is different to mine.'

He sniffs and clears his throat. 'I took you to dinner.'

'You did. Thank you. Now I need to get back to work.'

'Arc you seriously not going to come with me?' His volume rises.

'Are you seriously asking me that?'

He pauses, and when he continues, there's no energy behind his statement, but it still rouses my bile. 'The least you can do is come out with me one more time.'

'What? You think I owe you something?'

'That was a very expensive restaurant.'

'You have got to be kidding!' I'm pretty sure he isn't.

'Come on, Ella, just one more night. It'll be fun.' Now he sounds as if he's cajoling a five-year-old.

'Scott, let me be very clear. A woman does not owe you anything in return for a date. To even consider that she does is the epitome of chauvinism. And the mere suggestion of it will send any intelligent woman running for the hills. I'm an intelligent woman, Scott. Don't insult me.'

'Why, you little …'

My jaw actually drops. He must have turned away from the phone because his voice grows muffled, but I still get the gist of it: a string of curses. The intensity of his sudden anger rings a warning bell in my mind.

'I'm sorry you feel that way, Scott,' I say in my most placating voice. 'But I really don't think we're suited to each other. Go dancing. Have a great time and meet someone else who—'

'I don't want someone else. I want you.' He sounds like he's going to cry.

I'm speechless. Truly, what can you say to that?

'And you were a dancer; you must like dancing. Please, give me another chance,' he continues in that same sad tone. 'We just need to get to know each other better.'

'No. We tried that. At the restaurant. You did all the talking. You didn't even find out that I spent three years on a Buddhist retreat in the south of France. If you had, you might have realised that I'd moved on from nightclubs.'

'Then let's have coffee.' He doesn't sound hopeful—wise under the circumstances.

'No. I don't want to see you again. I'm sorry. Let's face it, we just didn't hit it off.'

'I can give you a good time, if you'll just let me.'

Ew! 'No, Scott. This is goodbye.' I slam the receiver back on its cradle with more force than necessary, and I stare at the phone until my heart returns to normal. I've turned guys down plenty of times before, but this time I feel as if I've narrowly escaped something … dare I say … dangerous. The relief is far too great for simply avoiding a long drive, sore feet, terrible music and bad company. I have no concrete reason to feel this way, but I feel it nevertheless. Woman's intuition, I guess. I hope it was wrong.

Either way, Scott is not my problem anymore.

With a click of my mouse, I open a Word document and re-enter Kelee's World.

27

Kelee's World

'Slade!' Kelee burst through the door into the dungeon.

The guards, heavy set with bristling beards, stood, their board game forgotten. One stood in front of her. 'Miss Menhir, you shouldn't be down here.'

'Stand aside, man.' She looked him in the eye and commanded him with all her passion.

'Your father would not like it.'

Kelee did not like his placating tone. She tried to duck around, but he blocked her way, his arms out, palms up.

She placed her hands on her hips, tilted her head, and narrowed her eyes. 'Father would not like you physically restraining me, but that's what you'll have to do if you want to stop me going in there. I'm sure if I spoke to him he would agree that I have a right to see a prisoner.'

The guard shrugged. 'Fine. It's on your head if it angers him.'

'I accept the responsibility.'

The guard clicked his heels together and bowed his head in the traditional Magan way, then stepped aside. Kelee nodded in return and walked on.

The second guard already stood by the cell room door. He unlocked it and pulled it open. He avoided her gaze, but couldn't hide the smirk on his face.

'What?'

He looked up and grinned. 'I knew he had no chance of stopping you, Miss.'

Kelee pressed her lips together as if annoyed, but her eyes twinkled and a smile broke out. The second guard repeated the bow and gestured her inside.

She shivered at the damp chill, and her nostrils flared at the smell of urine and unwashed bodies. She'd never been down here in her life, had never had a reason, and hoped she never would again. Cells fashioned from strong metal bars lined both walls. She raced down the walkway between them, scanning the occupants, a dangerous-looking bunch, but some looked so sickly that, regardless of their crime, they posed little threat to anyone now.

Slade sat on a bench against the back wall in the end cell, still in the clothes she'd borrowed for him for the ball, though well rumpled instead of finely pressed now. He stared at the floor, his posture one of defeat.

Tears moistened Kelee's eyes. 'Oh Slade, my love. I am so sorry. I can't believe this has happened.'

He sprang up and raced to the bars, a smile breaking through the grime on his face. He scrubbed a sleeve over his cheek, then looked at the sleeve and winced. 'I keep the stables cleaner than this place. I'm sorry about the suit.' He reached a hand through the bars, then pulled it back and gripped the bars. 'I long to touch you,' he explained, 'but I don't want to sully you with the dirt.'

Kelee smiled and stroked his face. His smile was as glorious as ever, and love filled his gaze. 'The charges are a joke; I'll get it all sorted out and get you out of here.'

The smile vaporised. He shook his head. 'It's no joke.'

'You didn't steal anything. I gave you the suit.'

'It's not the suit. They found Beak's mother's necklace in my pocket.'

Kelee's jaw dropped. She never doubted his innocence for a moment. 'That bastard!'

'He must have slipped it in when he grabbed me.'

'I'll get you out of here, I promise.'

He shrugged and shook his head. 'Didn't they tell you?'

'Tell me what?'

'The family have called for my death.'

'For stealing!'

'They have a right to demand whatever punishment they see fit.'

'I know the law, but father does not have to bow to their demands.'

'I suspect Beak will do his utmost to ensure that he does.'

Kelee sighed. He must have discovered their liaison. Slade nodded. She didn't like the resignation in his eyes. 'And I will do my utmost to ensure that he doesn't.'

'Of course, you will. But Beak's family has a great deal of power. Mine has none.'

'And mine is the most powerful family in this clan.'

'Do you think your father wishes you to marry a stable hand?'

Kelee swallowed. 'A stable hand with noble breeding.'

'But a stable hand nevertheless. Don't worry, I have lived each moment with you as if it were my last. I have no regrets.'

'Better dead than left in here to rot,' a voice croaked from a bundle of rags in the next cell.

Kelee looked into the cell. A bench and a bucket; just like the rest. She wondered if her mother knew of the conditions down here.

'I expect they think that if they make it too pleasant, it won't be much of a deterrent,' Slade said as if reading her mind.

'It can at least be clean.'

'Good luck with that.'

The man next door coughed. Another echoed the rasping sound from further down the room.

'You'd better go. It's not healthy down here,' Slade said, thinking of her before himself, as usual.

'I'll get you out, one way or another. I promise.' She grasped his hand and squeezed.

He squeezed back and lifted her hands to his lips.

'Aw, young love. 'Tis a sight for sore eyes,' the neighbour croaked.

Slade chuckled. 'I'm glad you find it entertaining.'

'Don't give up hope,' she said, pleading with her eyes.

'Hope breeds disappointment. Acceptance allows one peace regardless of what occurs.'

Kelee frowned. He sounded like Miramar. Was Slade a Warrior? She had suspected as much several times. If he were, then other Warriors would exist amongst the Menhirs, and she would have help even if all else failed. She smiled. Miramar would know.

'Go, before the chill enters your lungs,' he said and kissed her hand again.

28

Visitor

I stand at the sink and stare through the window into the night. My fridge is noisy. Or are all fridges like that, and you can just hear mine because of the silence? Silence in the bush isn't really silent though. Frogs croak from the pond. A ring-tailed possum yips. An owl hoots in the distance, and the late summer crickets sing, as always. A light breeze ruffles the leaves in the canopy, but stillness remains king of this night.

With a twist of the tap, I flush out the remains of the dish-washing water and face my evening. Much as I'd love to have a night off, I have to go back to the computer. I'd be able to finish the edit on Kelee's World in time without a problem if it hadn't been for Dita—and now Scott—wasting my time. But I expect I've seen the end of Scott; I've vowed to ignore anything else Dita sends my way, and I figure that a few long days will see me caught up on the job. With that in mind, I walk to my office with an optimistic step.

A flash of movement outside catches my eye. I freeze, senses alert, but whatever it was has already gone, so fast that I wonder if I'd seen it at all. I shake my head and continue walking. Perhaps a bat flew past.

Thump. Something bumps on the veranda, too high to be a wombat. I stop again and listen. Nothing. I swallow, my throat suddenly dry. It sounded like someone ran into a veranda post, but my closest neighbour lives a kilometre away, and why would they be here at this time of night skulking around my house? Perhaps their phone is out, but why didn't I hear a car, and why don't they have a torch? Everyone up here has a torch. The night is pitch black without street lights. A shiver runs down my spine. It can't be a person, and yet I can't shake the feeling that it is.

Dita can't turn up on my doorstep and abuse me as he does online. Or can he? I run my various profiles through my mind—I'm appalled at the number of them and I'm only thinking of the ones I actually use—but I'm pretty sure I've never left my actual address anywhere; the nearest town, yes, but not the street. He probably lives in America anyway, and even he wouldn't be crazy enough to get on a plane and come all the way here just to scare the daylights out of me. Would he? Nah. That's ridiculous.

I'm not going to open the door and ask if anyone is there, not like they do in movies. I'm not that stupid. No. I race around the house locking the doors and pulling curtains, and for the first time ever, I wish I had drapes on all the windows. Though I know it's extremely unlikely, I feel as if someone is watching me, and I am suddenly aware that I am a woman alone in the bush, kilometres from anywhere.

My brain does a quick inventory of the house for a weapon. Am I being paranoid, or just prudent? A knife would be far too dangerous. I could kill someone. Something heavy and blunt would be best, something I could knock someone out with. I try to imagine myself whacking someone on the head hard enough to do that. My arm and shoulder muscles contract as if practising, and, despite my vow of non-harming, I know that I could if I needed to—but only as a last resort. It doesn't surprise me that the image in my mind is a man, faceless, but definitely male. The closest thing I have is a frying pan. It's not heavy enough but I grab it anyway, creep into the lounge room, lit only by my reading lamp, and angle myself so I can see onto the veranda.

I suck in a breath. A man stands on my veranda silhouetted against the light shining from the kitchen. My heart pounds. He's peering inside, not knocking on the door as he should. For a rare moment, I don't know what to do, but I do know I need to do something. No way am I spending an evening with a feral human wandering around outside. And this guy is feral. Any normal person would have declared himself.

I grip the frying pan and walk into the family room. The light from the standard lamp exposes me to the stalker, and I don't like the feeling, but I keep moving. A light switch for the veranda sits on the wall beside the sliding door. I flick it on. Light floods the veranda. My jaw drops. Scott stands there shading his eyes against the sudden illumination.

I don't know whether to be relieved or angry, so both emotions battle for supremacy. I click the lock and slide the door open enough to stick my head out.

'Why are you skulking around my house in the middle of the night?' I make no effort to sound friendly.

'I've come to visit.' His eyes light up and he turns his charming smile on me—all confidence and energy today.

My stomach sours. 'Then why didn't you knock?'

He shrugs as if it's completely irrelevant. 'Just hadn't got around to it yet.'

That's a lie. 'I'm about to get an early night, so I'd appreciate it if you'd leave.'

'What? Can't I come in?' He's clearly scandalised by the idea. 'But I drove all this way just to see you!'

I frown; he's jiggling from foot to foot as if he's got extra energy to burn. Is he on something? 'I didn't invite you.' His puppy-dog eyes don't fool me. I recognise the lusty gleam from my stripping days. Instinct warns me to be careful. And I didn't hear a car. 'Where's your car?'

'I left it on the road. I wasn't sure what state your drive might be in after all the rain, and I didn't want to risk getting stuck.'

Or he didn't want me to hear him arrive. I remind myself that I've handled stroppy blokes before—but never alone in the middle of the bush. 'You walked down the drive without a torch?'

He flicks on a torch I hadn't noticed in his hand and shines it in my face. I throw a hand in front of my eyes and peer at him from beneath it. He's grinning at me like a mad man now, and there's definitely something feral in his eyes. 'Cut it out, Scott. I'm too tired for games. Seriously, just go home. I thought I'd made it clear that I didn't want to see you again.'

'Oh, go on, you didn't give me a chance. Give me thirty minutes, and I'll show you what you're missing.'

I frown; is this super-confident, self-assured man the same one I spoke to on the phone? Maybe he's high on something. 'Sorry, no. I really do need an early night. And you really do need to leave.'

'Oh yeah, sorry about that. I didn't mean to scare you.'

I don't believe him; he's grinning like it's a joke. 'Good night, Scott.' I slide the door shut, and hear him mutter on the other side.

'Stupid bitch.' He looked away, making it look like I wasn't supposed to hear it, but either he misjudged his volume or he wanted me to hear it every bit as much as Dita had wanted me to see his update on Facebook.

He looks up again with an attempt at a smile, but his jaw is tense and his eyes bulge slightly as if he's trying to stay in control, and he doesn't leave. I take a deep breath, tell myself that I can handle this, walk to the table, scoop up my phone and return to the door. I hold my phone up, point to it, and mouth police. His fake smile turns to a frown.

'If you don't go away now, I'll call the police,' I say loud enough for it to carry through the door.

Anger hijacks his expression. His eyes narrow and his lips curl into a sneer. But my words work. He turns, flicks on his torch and strides into the darkness.

Only then, as I watch the torch light shrink in the distance, do I realise how badly I'm shaking. I struggle to banish the look on Scott's face from my mind, and I can't stop a sinking feeling of dread. Safety here isn't just a matter of changing a password.

29

Lexie's Last Dance

Lexie took a deep calming breath. It didn't matter how many times she danced, butterflies always flittered around her stomach in the few moments before she stepped into the light. At least she didn't have to walk through the bar to get to the stage as she did in a couple of the venues. Going out wasn't too bad, coming back wearing only a g-string was torture. What you did on stage was an act. The pool of coloured light defined the stage and created a barrier between reality and fantasy that kept her safe. As soon as she stepped off the stage, reality came rushing back in. She became just another woman and all too touchable.

'Okay, lads, time to start the show,' Bob boomed over the PA. The room fell expectantly silent. 'Put your hands together for the beautiful and dynamic Miss Electra.'

They did, too, along with some wolf whistles. Lexie smiled. She loved these guys, loved their unadulterated enthusiasm and almost childlike delight in their weekly treat. She didn't love guys like The Creep though.

The music kicked in, hard and fast, and she stepped onto the stage flicking her riding crop into her hand. Thought vanished. Immediately immersed in the rhythm, Lexie's awareness both honed in on her body moving in space, and expanded to encompass the whole of the club. Performing was such a hit.

The character came naturally, an extension of the costume and hard-hitting music, and though playing it tough, she regarded the audience with smiling eyes, reminding everyone that this was a game. Bands played here on Saturday nights, so, unlike some of the venues, coloured lights gave the right atmosphere, and a flick of a switch plunged the audience into blessed darkness.

Lexie scanned the audience with laser eyes. Her ability to connect with them through the curtain of light gave her act an intimate feel. She danced for each of them. She loved each of them. She made them feel good. Their smiling, enraptured faces were a testament to her power. They loved her back. They would protect her with their life.

Except for guys like The Creep.

Lexie felt him hovering on the left-hand side, too close to the stage. She didn't go near him. One of the things she loved about stripping was the freedom of improvisation, no hours of rehearsing steps, and she could adjust her act to suit the venue. She had a character, a theme, and an intent for each song—a certain number of articles to remove until only a tiny g-string remained. No full nudity allowed. A year ago, some venues still insisted on pasties to cover her nipples. Such a joke.

Sal would bend over, bum to audience, and pull hers aside. 'They never see their wives' and girlfriends' fannies,' she'd told Lexie once. 'It's education they need to have.'

Lexie was happy to let Sal play anatomy teacher. Lexie just gave a royal command performance—though she couldn't imagine a strip tease artist ever being invited to perform for the Queen. This wasn't Covent Garden, the venue coveted by dancers the world over, not by a long shot, but no audience deserved less than her best, and the guys reciprocated her warmth and the sheer joy she brought to her work.

That's how she saw her role, not as titillation, not as something dirty and furtive, but as a sharing of pleasure in the human form, joy of the dance and artistry in bringing the two together in a way that delighted the senses and took the audience on an emotional journey that ended in something so intimate and fused with love that it transcended ordinary reality.

Sal's act was pornography. Lexie's was erotic art, but she made no judgement on which was best; they were just different.

But The Creep didn't see that. His energy sat like a lump of spiky lead in her radar. She sent him the same love, bathed him in the same purity of mind, but his hard shell would take someone with more guts than her to break through.

The music changed, and she ripped open her jacket, exposing the whole universe swirling live in her chest. In reality, all she exposed was her lacy push-up bra and a lot of bare skin barely shrouded by a sheer shirt tied at her waist above her fake leather—stretchy and Valcro-sided for easy exit—hot pants.

The men in the bar didn't know it, but Lexie was not just a stripper, not just an exotic dancer, she was a means to liberation.

She transported all except The Creep. His mind was too closed, too full of whatever abuse had caused his closed mind and mental brutality. For him, she represented merely an object to be abused and used, and the corrupt power of his intention battled with her purity.

A fight between good and evil took place that day, in that innocuous suburban pub. Miss Electra electrified the room, drove through their preconceptions like a semi-trailer through a plate glass window, and won the battle. Except for the one that got away.

She left the stage deep in thought and feeling somewhat soiled. She barely acknowledged Sal passing with a smile on her way to the stage. She'd been all too aware of the nature of The Creep's gaze. No matter how purely she saw herself and her act, she did not want to contribute to solidifying any man's derogatory thoughts about women.

Alone in the storeroom again, she folded her costume and prepared for the next act, but her mind dwelled elsewhere. Intelligence wasn't sufficient defence against a man twice her weight and strength, and that was all she had. What if he found her alone and raped her, as his gaze had? She could see the courtroom drama as plainly as if it had already happened on some alternate layer of reality. She's a stripper, they'd say, a whore—though she wasn't and never would be, and even if she was, why anyone thought that a woman's occupation gave a man permission for rape was beyond Lexie. Rape was rape. It meant violent non-consensual sex, so even if a woman said yes yesterday, if she said no today, she had said no. Poor communication was no defence, and yet they used it as if it were. She led me on, they'd say, got me fired up; I couldn't control myself. As if any of that was an excuse! She was not an evil temptress, and even if she was, she would never ask for rape.

Suddenly, Lexie felt vulnerable and naive. Mortal terror raced through her veins. Had she been blind and stupid? She waited for an answer, but none came. Her mind had gone blank, but gradually something emerged, not a thought, but a certainty about the future.

One more act to go and she would see if that retreat centre would give her a concession rate. She'd had enough of this battle.

She'd also ask Bob to ask Pete to walk her to her car.

30

At the Market

'He did what?' Liz asks, looking suitably scandalised.

'Played creepy guy.' I summarise, then watch the emotions flicker across her face as she processes the information.

We've finished setting up her market stall. Her wares are all beautifully displayed, and we have the obligatory morning coffee from the guy who doesn't do a half-bad coffee considering he dispenses it from a market stall. We're sitting on camping chairs behind a table covered in little clay sculptures. I've just told her about Scott's unscheduled visit.

'I'm really sorry,' she says finally. 'I had no idea he'd be like that.'

'How could you? You didn't know him.' I take a sip of my coffee and wrap my hands around the styrofoam mug to keep them warm. The sun hasn't hit our stall yet.

'You said he was okay on the date, just boring.'

I nod. 'That about sums it up.'

'Barbara said she saw you with him that night, said he'd asked her a couple of days earlier if she knew you, but he'd seemed angry, so she told him she didn't.'

I smile, pleased my old school friends are still looking out for me. 'He's just a little desperate to get a woman and doesn't take rejection well.'

Liz scoffed. 'Does anyone?'

I chuckle. 'He was apologetic though. But it was scary; he kind of flipped. I doubt I'll see him again though, not after threatening to call the police.'

'Maybe he's bipolar or something,' Liz suggests. It doesn't help. 'The sooner you move or get someone else to live up there with you, the better,' she adds and shoots a smile at the first customer who's browsing the new cute line. The woman takes a quick look at the three awesome masks on display behind us, then moves on.

I stare into the sky and enjoy a simple moment of being. The veil parts again and reveals the vibrancy at the core of our world. I see everything from the inside out. Everything—people, trees, stalls and goods, even the dust and stones underfoot—exist with the ease of a calm ocean, the unboundedness of the sky and the clarity of a lyre bird's call. I smile at the is-ness of it all, and my smile widens as I note that the super vibrancy is because everything is empty of is-ness as well. A dichotomy that would confound most folk, but for a Buddhist explains the very nature of existence. It's there, all right, just not in the way it appears.

'You're off with the fairies again,' Liz says.

'It's all about zeros and ones,' I reply. 'One is meaningless without zero.' I don't look at her, but I know she's rolling her eyes.

'I don't know how you can look at the sky and see binary code.'

I've tried to explain it to her before, but you can't fully understand it until you've experienced it— how something can be and not be at the same time and without any contradiction. And in order to experience it, you have to be able to part the veil of concepts. It takes a bit of meditation practice, but once you've got it, it's the best high ever.

'Excuse me,' a soft male voice with a hint of an English accent asks from behind me.

Liz looks up and smiles, then glances at me with wide eyes. 'Could you help the gentleman, please, Ella; I need to pop away for a moment.'

She's out of the stall before I have a chance to blink, so I turn to the customer and instead of the smile I thought I'd give, I go into a kind of shock and just stare. He stares back with a raised eyebrow, his warm brown eyes apparently questioning my sanity. I catch my lapse and blink myself back into normal operating mode.

'Sorry, I was away with the fairies.' Maybe I do believe in them after all. The man before me sure is pure magic.

He chuckles.

I tilt my head and check out the rugged face with its strong jaw, high cheekbones and straight nose.

I've seen those eyes, that disarming smile and that mop of sandy hair before.

'You were at Mark's engagement party, weren't you?'

I nod, far too delighted that he remembered, and also somewhat appalled at my teenage reaction.

'It was a good party. Did you enjoy yourself?'

'Thanks, yes, and you?'

He nods. 'My niece is having a birthday. She's in England, and I thought I'd send her something that says Australia without being tourist junk.'

'All this is perfect, and small enough not to cost a fortune to post.' I indicate the table with a sweep of my hand.

'I'm guessing she'll like these cute little guys.' He points at the new range.

'I reckon you can't go wrong with one of them.'

He grins, then says nothing as he looks carefully at each one. He's not tall, but taller than me, and I see muscles beneath the T-shirt.

I wait, wanting to connect with this man and wishing I could say something. But the silence remains. I have no idea what to say and curse my social awkwardness. Then I realise that my focus is so totally on him that everything else has faded into the distance. I'm back beneath the veil and he's there too—everyone's there, of course, they just don't know it, but I sense awareness in him. And clearly, he's as aware of me as I am of him. We don't need words to connect; we're already connected. We bathe in each other's awareness while he picks up each little statue, holds it in front of him and turns it around. The little smile remains on his face, and I have a feeling that he doesn't want this to end any more than I do.

He picks up the last statue. 'I'm waiting for one to jump out at me and say, yes, I'm right; take me, take me.'

I'm right. Take me.

He looks at me and his grin widens even further. 'I'll take this one.'

I nod. 'Good choice.' I take the clay figure from his hand, grab some tissue paper and wrap it, feeling his eyes on me all the while. I'm still stuck for words. I want to ask if he meditates. But how do you ask something like that? Besides, I know the answer; he has to. That kind of awareness doesn't come without a certain amount of attention to its development. We exchange money for goods. He could leave now, but he hesitates and looks at the masks behind me.

'They're amazing. Did you do them?'

I shake my head. 'My friend Liz is the artist. They're really cheap at that price.'

'I can see that.' His sun-streaked hair bounces when he nods. I assume that he surfs. 'They must take a lot of time. The expression on that one,' he points to the siren, 'is extraordinary.'

I smile, really glad he can see that.

'What do you do, then?'

I chuckle. 'When I'm not helping my friend out at the market, I'm an author and editor.'

He inclines his head with an appreciative and respectful expression. No, yeah-but-what-do-you-do-for-a-living attitude. I definitely like this guy.

'Fiction?'

Yay! He knows the word. I nod and feel like I'm grinning like an idiot, but I can't help it.

'Published?'

I nod again. Now I'm one of those bobble-headed dogs you see on the stalls at fairgrounds.

'Excellent. Well done. What's it called? What's it about?' His eyes are alight with curiosity.

'*Catnip Creek*, but the working title was *The Revenge of the Killer Dung Beetle*. The publisher thought it was too flippant.' I shrugged. I still reckon it would sell better with my name.

He opened his mouth to ask more, but before he could get a word out, a little girl ran over and started gushing over the cutesy stuff. Her whole family followed, all talking at full volume.

'Don't touch them!' The large woman with the puggish face slapped the girl's hand. 'If you break 'im, you'll have to pay for it.'

It didn't look like we'd get a sale out of this lot. I turned back to the mystery man. He opens his mouth again, but a loud American drawl interrupts. 'How much for the big one?' A chubby finger points at one of the masks on the stand behind me. The price is beside them, written large enough for a myopic toddler to read.

'Two hundred and fifty dollars. We can package it for safe shipping.'

'I'll give you a hundred.' She raises her grey eyebrows, blinks and purses her lips as if to say, 'You know that's all it's worth'.

'It's already discounted—a lot.' *Go to Asia if you want to bargain. It's that way.* I even tilt my head to the north—just slightly. She thinks I'm smiling at her, but actually I'm grinning at my silent humour.

'Hmf,' the woman replies and shuffles away, her enormous arse wobbling beneath her bum bag—oh, wait, it's a fanny bag in the States, isn't it? If they knew what a fanny was here ...

The elegant Englishman clears his throat. I turn back to him and nearly burst out laughing. He's chuckling silently, clearly enjoying the exchange. I wonder how much of my thoughts he read in my face.

'I'll take the mermaid,' he says. 'Wait ... no; it's a siren, isn't it?'

We are so definitely on the same wavelength. 'Yeah, elegant rather than cute; not so easy to find elegant stuff these days.'

He nods. Is that grief I glimpse in his eyes? Or nostalgia, perhaps? Does he miss England? He feels like an Aussie, and his accent is subtle. He's been here a long time. Who is this guy?

I get the art work down and wrap it while he wanders into town to the ATM. I'm amazed at how light it is. Liz's technical skills really are excellent. She returns as soon as he's gone, but though her eyes ask a million questions, we don't have time to talk, because a busload of tourists descends on the stall. The cute line runs out first, then they take the bunyips because they're so 'Orstarlian'.

Mystery man returns in the middle of the rush, and I'm so busy, I barely manage a nod. Liz takes his money, gives him his treasure, thanks him and bids him goodbye—no time for anything else. The tourists are jostling for a place at the front of the table. The good ones—by which they mean cute—are going fast, and no one wants to miss out. For some reason, we're the flavour of the day. I'm pleased for Liz; the money will encourage her to keep going, and the big sale will inspire her to make more that are truly art.

Damn it! I realise that I never got his name.

We sit down again. The rush is over, and the market is back to an ordinary Sunday crowd.

'You didn't get his phone number!' Liz says, her expression one of utter disbelief. 'He bought an art-work, for God's sake! Don't you know what a find that is?'

I shrug. 'It just didn't work out that way. Besides, he's probably married.'

'Looked to me like he was flirting with you.' She takes a swig of water from her bottle.

'He might have just been being polite too. It's hard to know with Englishmen.'

'Of which, you have enormous experience,' she said sarcastically.

'It wasn't just women in France, you know.'

She reaches over and pats my hand. 'He might come back later. Or next month.'

I nod and sigh, and reach for my laptop. Much as I'd like to give Liz the whole day, I've got a book to edit.

The English ex-pat doesn't return.

Kelee's World

Kelee stared out the library window into the stables' courtyard and sighed. Slade should be down there, but a boy of around ten years groomed her horse this morning. Kelee had never felt so little like riding in her life.

The door opened quietly. Kelee turned, holding her breath. The grey-haired healer walked across the dim room towards her, her traditional embroidered shirt swinging around her calves.

'Well? What did he say?' Kelee searched her mentor's face, but saw no hint of a smile. She let out a shaky breath.

Miramar gave an apologetic shrug. 'I tried, but I am Torrens Clan. Your father only tolerates me here because my healing is useful to him.'

Kelee silently cursed the split in Magan society that slotted clans into either the Mage or the Warrior Clan alliance. 'What did he say?'

Miramar wrapped a comforting arm around Kelee's shoulders and gave her a squeeze. 'He said that the passion you showed when begging for his release sealed the boy's death.'

'What?' Kelee wrenched herself from her mentor's hug. Tears filled her eyes. 'How could he?'

'Your father does not want you marrying a stable boy.'

'Noble blood runs in his veins!'

'Indeed, but Beak's father has Lord Menhir's ear, I'm afraid. He insists that you should not be the means for that family line to regain its honour.'

'I have not asked if I could marry him.'

'You don't have to, my dear. Your love is clear to all.'

Kelee grit her teeth. Was she that transparent? Apparently so.

'What does your mother say on this?'

Kelee buried her face in her hands. 'The same.'

'I am so sorry, Kelee. This matter burdens my heart.'

'They don't need to execute him!' Kelee's voice rose to fever pitch. 'I can promise never to see him again.' Even exile had to be better than death. But could she keep such a promise? No, she would travel beyond the realm to find him.

Miramar nodded and sat on the couch, patting the space beside her. 'Come, child, nothing will be gained by upsetting yourself further. We must not give up hope. Who else can we bring to your cause? What about your brother?'

Kelee shrugged and slumped down beside the older woman. 'He left right after the ball. He doesn't even know. And no one knows where he has gone. As usual. And what can he do, anyway? Slade has no word other than his own for his innocence, yet three men were with Beak when he found the jewels in his pocket.'

Miramar sighed. 'Execution is an unusually harsh punishment for theft, especially where such theft cannot be proven without a doubt.'

'Father believes Beak because he is family. Who do you believe?'

Miramar turned a steely gaze on Kelee and spoke with a Warrior's power. 'Beak has a dark heart. Slade has a pure one.'

Goosebumps rose on the back of Kelee's neck at the surety in her tone. 'Are there Warriors amongst the Menhirs?'

A smile blossomed across the old healer's face. 'Of course, my dear. Many families in the Mage clans stuck to the old ways after the split, and there are many in the Warrior clans who care more for magic than enlightened awareness. They do not announce their beliefs, of course, but no one can prevent them from having them.'

Kelee swallowed. 'Would … would you know how to contact them?' she whispered.

Miramar's eyebrows rose, and Kelee realised that she had just suggested that there might be some kind of Warrior underground amongst the Menhir clan.

Participation in such a thing would be treason, and the punishment for treason was execution.

'I'm ... I'm sorry. Forget I asked. I just thought they might help.'

'I'm sure they would, my dear.' Miramar patted her hand. 'I will talk to your mother. Perhaps I can convince her that exile would be a more reasonable course.'

'She would still have to convince Father.'

'She will see that siding with you on a compromise will regain her a measure of your goodwill.'

Kelee nodded, but she had little faith in her ailing mother. She was often too sick to leave her bed. 'If all else fails, I will break him out.'

Miramar's eyes widened. 'And how, my dear, would you do that?'

Kelee shrugged and shook her head.

'Talk to his brother,' Miramar said quietly. 'He may already have a plan.' She stood then and wandered toward the table. 'Come, we have lessons to attend to.'

Kelee followed, hope blossoming in her heart. Of course, Slade's brother would have a plan. But how could Miramar know? Perhaps there really was a Warrior network here. Kelee hoped so. Her beloved's life quite likely depended on it.

What is it with these guys? I look up from my computer, suddenly realising that I'm thinking about Scott. His desire for me and his clumsy overtures are reminiscent of Beak and his pursuit of Kelee. And now he's getting in the way of my concentration on my work! I turn my awareness onto my feelings and discover a festering concern that perhaps I haven't seen the end of him. I stare at the feeling with my inner eye and it shatters like ice beneath a hammer.

32

Email Action

Another email with Dita as sender lurks in my inbox. I swore I would not open another from him, but curiosity wins. I can't resist. It's just words, I tell myself; I can handle it.

I click.

Email accounts are easy to break into. All your friends will be exposed. If you care for them, take the review down.

I drop my head into my hands and groan. I have to calm myself with steady breaths, but I'm glad I checked the email—forewarned and all that. I'm not angry, it's just getting tiresome now. Perhaps I should just take the review down, but principles are at stake here—mine. No, I won't bow to the bully. He will get sick of hounding me eventually. In the meantime, I just have to do what has to be done.

I change the passwords on my various email accounts and google how to block someone's emails from showing up in my box. While the results are loading, I browse some more emails. There's one from Tanya Kahn, Kelee's author:

I grit my teeth. I can't reply right now—my annoyance would likely flavour my words. I decide that deleting an email is less time consuming than learning how to do it automatically. Dita's interruptions don't just take time, they take away from the focus I need to get this work finished by the deadline. I have to shake the irritation out of me before I can settle back to work.

I turn on some dance music—loud. After five minutes of throwing myself around to the beat, I feel much better, but I can't stop the feeling that my life is turning into a bad novel.

Merlin jumps onto my lap and gives me a smooch. I give him a cuddle and bury my face in his fur. He purrs, and though I'm holding him in my arms, this trusting little creature embraces my heart with a big hug.

Tring tring.

Damn; I was just about to start work.

Tring tring.

I lift the receiver.

Silence.

I'm about to put it down, thinking it's a call centre, when the caller speaks.

'I really need to see you again.'

I can barely hear him, but I recognise the voice. 'I'm sorry, Scott, but you lost all chance of that when you crept around my house in the dark two nights ago.'

'Look, I'm really sorry about that.' He actually does sound sorry. 'I was a bit reckless that night. I should have phoned first. Sometimes, I … I get inspired and forget that others … '

'Look, I'm sure you'll find someone else, just, next time, try to think about the woman sometimes, about what they might like. It'll help a lot.'

When he speaks again, it's in a small, sad voice. 'I … I don't want someone else … I want you.'

I shiver. I don't want this guy fixated on me. I have to be hard. 'But I don't want you. You think only of yourself.'

'So do you. I know I shouldn't have come without calling first, but … if you thought about me, you'd have let me in.'

He pauses again—an uncomfortable silence— but I take the time to think. The level of my self-obsession is always worth checking, but no, thinking of others doesn't mean you let them walk all over you. A relationship with this guy would end in pain for both of us. It already is painful. The anxiety of that night floods back.

'How about another dinner?' He doesn't sound too hopeful.

'It's too late for that, Scott.'

'I won't talk about myself at all, I promise … I mean … what's left to say, anyway.'

I ignore the sense of worthlessness I hear in his words, and focus on the whiny child aspect. He needs a firm hand for both our sakes. 'Creeping around someone's house in the dark is called stalking, and it's not right.'

'I didn't stalk you! I came up for a cup of coffee.'

'Oh yeah, that's right. It was my fault I got scared.' My voice takes on a steely tone.

'Don't patronise me.' Even from the other end of the phone line, I can feel Scott's anger rising. I have a sense of it pushing against some blockage, and I don't want to be around when it blows. 'I'll be seeing you again,' he says in a tone that's far too determined.

'Don't come here. I'll call the police if you do.'

'Don't you dare. That's not fair. They don't understand. I'll … I'll … I'll call you when I feel better.'

'Don't. Please. It's not—'

Click.

'—good for either of us.'

He hung up on me! I stand and begin to pace, too agitated to settle back to work. Scott's unpredictable behaviour is scary. *When I feel better?* Is something wrong with him? I nod. Yep, something isn't quite right. And, frankly, I don't want to know what it is. I just want him to go away and never come back.

Merlin jumps onto my desk, bunts me and meows. I scoop him up and carry him to the bedroom, where I lie down and close my eyes. I worked far too late on Kelee's World last night.

33

Clearing the Shed

An old wooden shed covered in spider webs and vines stood before her. Only a few grimy shards of glass remained in the shattered windows, and the door hung twisted from one hinge.

The woman who wasn't Ella, but was, took a deep breath and strode towards the building, then stopped at the threshold, anxious about what she might find inside. The shed was long overdue for a clean, but snakes and poisonous spiders could lurk amongst the junk—which was why she had put it off so long. Now she couldn't bear it any longer. The junk weighed her down, and she focused on that fact far too much. She needed to be rid of it. Really rid of it.

She poked her head inside and peered into the gloom. Dust tickled her nose and she sneezed. Her eyes adjusted to the lower light level, and the full glory of the mess revealed itself. Boxes overflowing with papers lay higgledy-piggledy against one wall. A rusted bicycle with flat tyres lay on top of them. A broken chair and a mirror pitted with age leaned against another wall, and a large cardboard box of old computers filled one corner. In the middle of the small space, rags escaped a tin chest too small to contain them, and countless reinforced stripy plastic bags held all number of unknown and unwanted items. A thick layer of dust covered everything. Not-Ella wanted to turn and run, but instead, she grimaced and stepped across the threshold.

The temperature dropped. Not-Ella shivered and looked around. Her mother's curtains spilled from one bag, another held an assortment of old shoes—her tatty point shoes lay on top, and a well-worn pair of high stilettos, complete with diamantes glued to their straps, lay beneath them. A shredded tutu, leg warmers and various stripping costumes filled another. Tatty books and magazines strained against the confines of another, and old photo frames peeked from the top of yet another.

Not-Ella reached into the nearest and least-dusty bag, and pulled out a wad of A4-sized con-certinaed paper. She squinted at the typed words on the top and winced at the content. The paper unravelled in pleats, and she fed it through her hands, scanning the words and shaking her head at the all too familiar garbage. Twitter. Facebook. Linked In. Emails. You Tube. Blog. Wordpress. Reviews. Authors. Dita. Tirades of angry words. Words leapt from the pages and swirled around her head. Thick fonts, script fonts, plain fonts, 9 point, 12 point, 36, 72 and larger, all danced around her screaming their words.

She dropped the paper and covered her ears, but the words were as much inside as outside. They flew around her like flies on a humid day, and at the same time, battered against the inside of her skull. She batted the words away from in front of her face and stared around with wide eyes. No way could she clean this out piece by piece. It would take ages and the words would drive her crazy long before she reached the last box. But the screaming had to stop.

She grabbed a box of paper and spilled its contents on the floor. Words flew from the papers like dust motes. She heaved another box on its side and kicked the papers until she'd spread them all over the floor. Words buzzed around her like angry bees threatening to sting. She ran from the shed.

A jerry can of petrol appeared at her feet. She carried it to the shed, splattered its contents on the walls and doused the papers inside. The words shrank from the fumes, then regrouped and attacked; their spiky edges cut into her flesh. She fled the shed, struck a match and threw it inside.

It flew in slow motion while Not-Ella backed away. A moment later, the shed exploded into flames.

Not-Ella sat on the cool grass with the heat of the flames on her face and watched her garbage burn.

Actual Ella awakes refreshed, but finds she's slept for far too long.

34

Kelee's World

Kelee took a deep breath and steeled her nerves, then flounced down the steps to the dungeon, bringing her feminine wiles to the fore. The two guards at the bottom, the younger man being one of those who'd let her pass before, looked up from their game and stood when they saw the identity of the visitor.

The elder one, his face grave in the light of the oil lamp, shook his head. 'No one is allowed down here at night, Miss Menhir. Standing rules, can't break 'em, even for you.'

'It's not night anymore; it's morning.'

He raised his eyebrows as if to ask if she thought him stupid. 'Still dark, Miss.'

'Dawn is breaking. I couldn't sleep. Please. I have to see him.'

He grimaced and peered up at the small barred window. The tiny patch of sky showed the first traces of dawn. 'I strongly advise against it.'

Kelee sniffed back tears. 'He's due to die this time tomorrow.' If she failed today, that would be true. But she would not fail. She could not.

'Aw, go on, Craken, let the young lady say fare-well to her love,' said the younger guard. ''Tis a sad thing, Miss. I feel for you.'

'You're too soft, Donic,' the elder scoffed.

Kelee drew two bottles of Menhir family beer from beneath her cloak and placed them on the table.

'Thankee, Miss Kelee; my throat is right parched, it is,' said the younger guard.

The elder's eyes twinkled and a slight smile tugged at the corners of his mouth as he surveyed the finest, most expensive beer in the whole of the Magan lands.

'Mother gave her permission for the visit.'

'But not your father, aye,' the elder said, raising his eyebrows.

'I never asked him.'

The younger guard chuckled but stopped abruptly at the glare of the other. 'What? Would you risk asking?' he asked the elder. 'The girl is smart. I say we let her in. Her father need never know.'

The elder guard's jaw tightened. He regarded her with a steely gaze for a moment, then nodded curtly. The younger grabbed the keys, unlocked the door to the cells and gestured her through the door. Both guards gave the customary bow and click of their heels as she passed.

'Thank you,' she whispered. 'This means a lot to me.'

The men smiled and closed the door. She noted with satisfaction that, as before, they did not lock it behind her. Her breathing eased; step one achieved. She took a moment to peek back through the small barred window and smiled when she saw the younger guard flip the top on the beer, take a swig, then hand the bottle to the other. The older guard hesitated, then shrugged and took the bottle. Kelee smiled; step two achieved. She wondered if the younger was a hidden Warrior. Knowingly or not, he'd helped move the plan along.

She turned and faced the corridor of cells. The damp air seared her lungs, and the smell made her nose wrinkle. She took a shallow breath and, ignoring the shadowy figures in the inhabited cells, strode to the last cell.

'Slade,' she whispered to the heap curled up on the bench at the far side of the cell.

He stirred, then sat up and rubbed his eyes. The few torches on the walls gave little light, and she couldn't see his expression until he drew close to the bars, then her heart leapt at his smile. His eyes retained their clarity and he seemed at peace.

'Are you a Warrior?' she whispered. Who else could face their death with such equanimity? Or did he know she would come for him?

His smile widened further. He nodded and calmly met her gaze.

Her heart leapt again. She glanced back at the door and refocused on her task. 'I've been talking to Flint.'

Slade nodded at his brother's name and drew closer.

'The guards should be asleep soon,' she whispered. 'We're getting you out. You'll have to leave the Menhir lands, but I'm coming too.'

His jaw dropped. 'Your father will never let you go.'

'By the time he realises, we'll be long gone, and we're going to Sheldra; even my father wouldn't seek me there.'

'Sheldra? You plan to become a Warrior?'

She nodded.

'I like this plan.' He reached through the bars and stroked her face.

She reached up, took his hand from her cheek and squeezed it. 'Flint has horses outside with saddle-bags packed. We just have to get to them without being seen.'

'Excellent. I'll follow you.'

She pulled a bundle from beneath her cloak and pushed it through the bars. 'Put this on; I'm getting the key.'

He chuckled quietly. 'That will help.'

Kelee smiled and tiptoed back down the cell-flanked corridor. Her smile faded when Slade coughed behind her.

'Can I come too?' the man in the next cell asked.

She ignored him.

Some of the other prisoners stirred as she passed, as if they knew something was going on. But they would have to stay behind.

Kelee was freeing a man wrongly accused; she knew nothing of the others and would not anger her father further by letting all kinds of criminals escape. Lord Menhir may be harsh sometimes, but she loved him anyway and did not cherish the prospect of leaving her comfortable life and not seeing her family again. Who knew what she would find in Sheldra?

Miramar had assured her that the Warriors would look after her and not hold her status as the daughter of the feared leader of the Mage Clan Alliance against her, but … she couldn't stay here after this even if she wanted to. She'd declared herself the wrong-doer when she'd handed the drugged beer to the guards.

She peered through the window in the door to the cells and smiled. The guards lay with their heads on their hands, their eyes closed. The elder one snored. Step three achieved.

Kelee opened the door slowly and, careful to make no sound, lifted the cell keys from their hook on the wall, then, clutching them tight, she walked back down the corridor, restraining the desire to run. Flint had stressed the importance of not stirring up the other prisoners. The last thing they needed was a ruckus in the cells.

The prisoner next door coughed as the door unlocked with a satisfying click. Step four achieved.

'Thanks,' Kelee whispered as she and Slade strode past his cell.

'Happy to help,' the man whispered back.

Kelee hoped he wouldn't spend too long in this dismal place.

They closed the outer door behind them and Slade turned the key in the lock as Kelee placed the cell door key back on its hook. The guards never stirred. Step five achieved. Now came the hard part.

Kelee led Slade through the lower corridors of the Menhir mansion, steering clear of the kitchen and other areas where servants were stirring. They ducked under the stairs to hide from a kitchen hand, and Kelee yanked Slade into a storeroom to avoid a footman, but five minutes after leaving the cells, they stood at the side door.

Kelee pressed her lips together. They'd taken too long. Dawn was upon them, and step six still had to be achieved. They had to walk across the open area to the gate behind the stables and into the wooded area where their horses waited, and they had to do it without raising suspicion or drawing the attention of the guards that randomly wandered the perimeter of the property.

Slade drew the hood of the embroidered velvet cape Kelee had given him over his head.

'You have to walk like a girl,' she told him.

'Yeah, I get it.'

Kelee slipped her arm through his and set off across the lawn towards the stables, her heart pounding. Slade patted her arm and whispered in a high voice:

'We shall have a lovely ride today, dear friend. And we shall leave all this sadness behind.'

Kelee nodded, her throat too dry to speak.

'It will be a beautiful day,' Slade continued.

Kelee nodded and hoped his words would be prophetic. Slade often helped calm her by drawing her attention to the simple things around her, and she appreciated it now, but she wished he wouldn't speak. He didn't really sound like a girl, but she couldn't shush him now, they were almost at the stable doors.

'Bit early for a ride, isn't it, Miss Kelee?' the head groomsman called as they walked past the open doors.

'I'm not riding now, thanks, Jordon.' Why did he have to pick today to be at work at the crack of dawn?

'Later, then.'

'Perhaps.'

Slade looked at the ground, tucked his hands beneath his cloak and pulled it over his boots, but apart from a quizzical frown at Kelee's companion, Jordon paid them no attention and went back to oiling the harness. The smell of horse and linseed oil wafted out of the doors.

They made it to the side gate before everything went wrong.

'Almost there,' Kelee whispered as they stepped through the gate.

'Good morning, Miss Kelee, who is your tall friend?' a voice asked from the ground beside the gate.

Kelee and Slade turned to the voice. One of Beak's men lounged against the rock wall. He climbed to his feet, his narrow eyes fixed on Slade. Slade grabbed Kelee's arm and hurried her towards the woods.

'Beak!' the man called. 'Over here.'

Beak emerged from the woods before them. A smirk spread across his face.

'What are you doing here at this hour?' Kelee asked.

'I was about to ask you the same thing.'

Kelee bit her lip and forced herself not to engage in a pointless debate. Clearly, he was there because he'd suspected that she would be too. 'Katiah and I are going for a walk,' she finally said in a wavering voice. She squeezed Slade's arm, warning him not to speak.

'Please introduce me.' Beak raised his eyes in challenge.

Kelee shook her head and moved to walk around him, but his hand shot out and grabbed her. Slade pushed her aside and punched Beak square in the jaw. His hands flew up, releasing Kelee, and the couple ran for the trees. A crack of wand fire sounded behind them, followed by the smell of singed dirt.

'Get the horses,' Beak yelled.

Slade threw back his hood and they raced through the trees. 'The old well,' Kelee whispered.

'This way,' Slade said and led her into a thicket too dense for horses to follow.

Branches ripped at her clothes and scratched her face, but still she ran. Horses hooves thundered on both sides of their thicket, and men shouted each time one of them glimpsed the fugitives.

'We should split up,' Slade said.

'No, they won't dare hurt me. Stay close and they can't risk a shot.'

Slade glanced her way. He didn't look too sure. They both knew it depended on the skill of the wand wielder. Wands were notoriously unpredictable, particularly at close range, but neither of them knew Beak's capacity. No matter. They still had to run.

Wand fire broke out when they drew near the well. Flint and his team held Beak and his men at bay while Kelee and Slade scrambled from the thicket and mounted the waiting horses.

Step six achieved!

They galloped off.

Hooves thundered after them.

Kelee let Slade take the lead. If they wanted him, they'd have to get past her first. Unfortunately, they did. One of their pursuers rode wide and attacked from the side. Slade's horse went down, screaming, a hole burned in his knee, another in his flank. Slade threw himself off as the horse fell.

Kelee slowed enough for him to spring on behind her, and though the horse stumbled briefly with the added weight, he galloped on. They made it to the main road where the plan had been speed, but top speed wasn't possible with one horse carrying both of them. Flint must have done a good job of holding Beak's men because only one followed. But one was all it took.

The crack of wand fire grew closer. Kelee passed her wand to Slade. They'd left one on his horse for him, but she figured it was still there. She felt him turn and heard the crack, then he slumped onto her.

'Slade!' she cried. Her heart shattered at the smell of burning flesh. No. Please. No.

His arms wrapped around her. 'Damnation,' he muttered.

Kelee dug her heels into the horse's flanks and grabbed the wand before it fell from Slade's loosening grip. She twisted around and sent a volley of wand fire at their rapidly gaining pursuer. To her dismay, the horse fell, not the man, but they left him pinned beneath the flailing beast and made their escape.

She didn't dare stop until she'd left Menhir Lands, then she turned off the main road, cantered along a narrow track and slowed to a walk. By the time she reached the hidden cottage, Slade's breath felt weak against her neck and he could barely maintain his grip around her waist.

Miramar and a Magan with a white cloak, marking him as from the Warrior Alliance, rushed from the cottage and helped her get Slade off the horse and inside.

He groaned as they laid him on a soft rug on the floor on his side, exposing the deep burn in his back to Miramar's scrutiny. The power of the blast had shattered bones and exposed organs. The healer tut-tutted, gave orders to the Warrior man to boil water and bring bandages, then she rummaged in her bag, withdrew various pouches and took them into the kitchen.

Kelee cradled Slade's head on her lap and stroked his damp hair off his forehead. 'Stay with me, Slade. Hang on. Miramar will heal you.' She couldn't find the certainty she needed to keep her voice steady.

Even then, despite his pain, his eyes maintained their peace and clarity. Their liquid depths drew her in and she felt his love wrap around her like a warm embrace. His lips tried to form words but couldn't.

'I know,' she whispered. 'I know. I love you too.'

He managed a faint smile, then he released one last ragged breath and the light in his eyes went out.

Darkness closed in around her. She refused to let him go, and her tears would not cease. She had given up her family and her home and had still lost him. Her heart wrenched apart and a great upwelling of anger burst out.

'Nooo!' she cried.

No.
This was not her story. This was not how it ended. She would not allow it to be.

35

Conversation with Kelee

I suck in a breath, expel it forcefully and sniff back tears. I can't believe the author did that. Wow. I was so totally with Kelee in that scene, so invested in her life that I shared her devastation at Slade's death.

I check the word count. I'm only seventy percent of the way through! That's far too early to kill off a main character, particularly such a handsome, noble one. Besides, I thought this was a romance, and you simply do not kill off the lover in a romance. It's just too depressing. Romance readers would hate it. I hate it.

I can't understand why the author has done it or where the story could go from here.

On a positive note, it was completely unexpected, making the story unpredictable, and that's usually a good thing, but … it doesn't feel right here. Still, I'm not the author and I have a job to do; I'll work on and see if she can resolve this without leaving Kelee and the reader completely crushed. Some authors like sad endings though; some readers do too, but a happy ending is an unwritten contract between authors and readers in romances. Slade's death has huge consequences in marketing this book.

I stare at my computer screen, shaking my head.

Maybe he isn't really dead.

I scan the next few pages and discover that no, Miramar does not bring him back to life. Kelee returns home to give him a proper funeral amongst his family. It's all so sad. Why? I ask myself. What purpose does his death fill in this story?

I return to the point where Kelee cries, 'Nooo!' and wonder if it needs the exclamation mark since the author says that she cries the word. I figure Kelee would go for the exclamation mark.

I felt like that once, but the death was my father's, not my lover's. The memory washes over me, but I don't dwell on it. I look out the window into the bush and raise my eyes to the sky. The grey clouds and impending rain are right for my mood.

The veil between the worlds parts once again and my mind merges with the very essence of the universe. My sombre mood dissipates in that space.

It's just a story, I remind myself.

No, it's not JUST a story. It's my story, and she got it wrong. Slade did not die.

My eyes widen, and I glance behind me. Merlin strolls in with that earnest look on his face. He stops and looks up at me. I note the colour co-ordination of the cream cat on the polished wood floor. Nice. But that wasn't his voice.

You have to change it. Make him not die.

I turn back to the computer screen, half expecting to see words typing themselves across the page, but no; this is reality, not fiction.

Your fiction. My reality.

Kelee. I smile.

I tried to tell her, but she wouldn't listen. She thought he had to die or I wouldn't get the burning desire to become a Warrior. But I went to Sheldra with him, and he, not his death, inspired me to start the training.

So that's why she turned up at Sheldra in book three of the *Diamond Peak* series. This spin-off story had to end up with her there. Alone. Because Slade wasn't in *Demon's Grip*.

He didn't have to be there. I was training with Ariel, and he was already trained. He doesn't have to be dead.

What about the rest of this story? Has she got it right?

She wrote the trials I went through to get to Sheldra true enough, but my grief was for the loss of my family. I felt I could not go back after helping him escape. But Slade was with me through those events. His support was the support of a Warrior, and that was my inspiration to take the training, not the bleak despair she wrote it as. You have to change it. Make it true.

I'm the editor, not the author. I can only make suggestions.

Isn't the inspiration gained from another's example a more noble motivation than that of simply wanting to get out of one's misery?

I shrugged. Misery is more dramatic.

Writer's artifice! A good writer can make inspiration as powerful as misery, and surely, reality is stronger than fiction.

Reality? I'm talking to a figment not of my imagination but of the author's imagination. And my imagination is creating this conversation because I don't like Slade's death.

I am NOT a figment of an author's imagination; she has merely discovered my story and written it down. I am as real in my world as you are in yours. Our worlds touch in the open plane of existence from which creativity springs. That is where she found Diamond Peak and the stories of those who dwell there, but her unearthing of my story has been flawed by her own limitations. The real story is richer than she can imagine.

You sound like a Warrior.

I can't see her face, at least not physically, but I know she smiles, and I realise that she is indeed a Warrior, and a powerful one at that. She's grown older and come a long way since the events of the book I'm currently editing.

She chuckles, and her presence grows stronger. *You have the openness to see my story in its entirety.*

See.

My eyes see the bush and the grey sky. My body feels solid in my office chair. I smell the spring jasmine and hear Merlin meow. And my mouth feels dry. And yet I do see her, and I do see her story and the many others that touch hers. We stand together in a twilight world of shifting light forms. My body here beneath the veil is light and unfettered by corporeal existence. I could go anywhere with a thought, but I stay focused on Kelee.

Her beauty far surpasses that written in the book I've been editing. Her long black hair has a blue sheen. Her vivid green eyes penetrate to the depth of my being, and she has a glow about her and an elegance of being that comes only with great wisdom. She wears the traditional maroon robes of a Magan sage.

I am not the same as I was then.

I nod. This place is timeless.

She waves her hand in an arc between us. The motion leaves a trail of smoke that dances before my eyes, and her story reveals itself to me in an instant. I see it all in one glance. It's a story that should be told.

That's why she found it. There is much in it to inspire others, but her limitations diminish its power. Yet, you see it all. You must help her write it as it should be written.

That's my job as an editor. But she may not listen to me.

You must try.

I'll present the alternative, but she may see it as my idea, and not want to do it simply for that reason.

Attachment to Ego is the cause of all problems.

I grin at the Warrior's lore.

Slade must not die. Her eyes take on a steely glint, and I get the feeling that there may be some repercussions in her world should the wrong story be published here.

If she does not change it, I will make sure that no one reads it.

I raise my eyebrows, but though I could ask a million questions, I say nothing. No matter how illogical or impossible it may sound, I don't doubt she could reach through the veil and sabotage the publication. It's all too easy for books to sink to the bottom of the pile of the many titles available. The causes and conditions for success are many and, like a stack of sticks, can be easily dismantled with the removal of one key element at the appropriate time.

Slade must not die. Promise me.

I'll do my best.

Kelee vanishes, and the veil snaps shut, returning me to ordinary reality.

I wonder how I'll deliver on my promise, then realise that, having seen the real story, in my mind Slade is alive and well, and the truth of his life is so vibrant that it overshadows the fiction. The book I'm editing now seems shallow. It lost its integrity with Slade's death. Readers will hate it. It won't sell.

I open my browser and begin writing an email to the author.

36

A Fragile World

I'm about to turn off the computer but decide to check my emails again first. I'm hoping for a 'yes' from the author who has been pussyfooting around the idea of having his book properly edited. I need the job. He needs the job done too. I'm just waiting for him to decide whether or not his book is worth the investment. It is, but he has to come to that understanding himself. Anything I say could be seen as suspect.

I scan my inbox and my heart spikes at the subject of an email. But it's not a good spike. There's nothing from the above-mentioned author. This one bears Dita's stamp.

Final warning.

DELETE, I tell myself. Don't look at it. I swore I would not read any more emails from the poor sod. But I do. Damn, stupid woman. I can't resist a peek. What if it's something I can act against before it happens, like the email hack threat?

TAKE YOUR REVIEW DOWN, OR I'LL TAKE YOU DOWN.

I recoil—literally. I push back in my chair and the wheels slide over the polished-wood floors without a sound while I shake my head in disbelief. I can't believe it: how dare he? It's ridiculous. He's like a child throwing a tantrum, and I am not going to cave in to his stupid antics. If anything, it makes me even more determined to keep that review where it is.

The last light flees from the sky and the heavens choose that moment to unleash a torrent of rain and cast my office into darkness. The universe has a wry sense of humour.

What is this guy planning now? I wonder. A flurry of abusive scenarios laced with fear race through my mind. No. I will not bow to a bully, and I will not let him destroy my peace of mind—but he already has … I have got to get rid of him! The thought throws my helplessness back in my face, and I grit my teeth. What can I do?

Delete. Report. Ignore.

This time, I make sure I won't ever see another email from him. I do a quick web search for how to block unwanted emails and learn about creating filters. I follow the steps and set it to send Dita's emails straight to the trash. It's a relief to know that I won't have to battle with myself over whether to look at his emails again.

Mental calm I can do something about.

The screen glows stark white in brilliant contrast to the night that has crept into my office. This rectangle of light is a window into an electronic world that has no real substance, only what we give it in our minds. Dita cannot touch me here in my real world. The only damage he can do is to my reputation, and then only so far as it exists online. My reputation is not me. It does not even exist as a tangible entity. The me he abuses is merely an electronic reflection of an ephemeral I.

I turn off the computer and smile as Dita's world fades from view. All it takes is one touch and he's gone.

Take that, arsehole.

I reach for the light and switch it on. The darkness dissolves instantly, like anxiety in the light of awareness. I stretch, then wander into the kitchen to prepare dinner.

Crash!

Boom!

Thunder shakes the house, vibrates through the old floorboards and widens my eyes. It's right above me. I stare out the window into the suddenly wild night.

Lightning flashes bright against the night and illuminates the grey sheets of rain pouring from the sky. It's as heavy as if a giant decided to empty a bucket over the house. The rain thumps on the tin roof and, in the background, the creek roars as the water rises—a barrage of sound. Merlin sits curled up in his basket. He lifts his head and stares through the window. His eyes widen as a flash of light turns the garden silver and another crash of thunder shakes the house. I won't be going shopping tomorrow. The flood-way will be impassable.

The lights go out. Damn. Some tree over the lines, no doubt. And my torch is a good stumble away. I move in time with the lightning, thinking how helpful having no curtains is right now. I don't need them up here in the bush. Curtains would just close me off from the beauty that surrounds my house; and only wombats, wallabies and birds are around to look in. The feral goats don't come close enough.

I grab the torch from its recharge station. There'll be nothing in the wires to recharge it until the SES sort out the tree and the power people fix the lines. I shine it on the floor and wander into the studio to enjoy the view. The floor to ceiling windows reveal the full glory of the storm. Jagged lightning, pounding out a rhythm between flashes in its sheet form, skips over the treetops and pirouettes off rocks, while rain and wind jerk the strings on puppets of shining leaves. The windows remind me of a series of huge video screens showing a slightly different version of the same event—the power of the natural world. For all that humankind can do, we're still at the mercy of storms and floods, drought and disease, earthquakes and tsunamis.

Eventually, I wander back to the living room and light a candle; it flickers into life, sending its golden glow into the room. Merlin watches me from his bed.

'What?' I say.

He yawns, stretches his front paws, then settles down for a nap.

I carry the candle into the bathroom and turn on the shower, grateful that it's gas with a pressure-operated ignition system—no electricity needed—and as I go through the motions of showering, I realise how fragile this modern world is.

Without electricity, everything falls apart.

Light, heat, transport, food storage, communications, manufacturing; all are reliant on this one thing—our Achilles heel. It wouldn't take much to bring us down. A huge solar flare would plummet our world into chaos.

And without electricity, my options for distraction from my concern are virtually nil. I take my time over making, eating and clearing away after dinner. Dita pops into my mind periodically, but I banish him by focusing on my activity. I let his image—the gravatar of a cartoon dog that he uses online—fade, thrust aside by relegating him to the not-worth-my-attention category.

But the end of my chores leave me nothing to hide behind. I wander into the studio again and watch the display. He's not worth my attention, but he batters against my consciousness until he gets it. What can he do that he hasn't already done? Time eclipses everything anyway, I remind myself. Posts and comments disappear from our screens as they slide down the time-lines. As long as we don't respond, they'll fade from public awareness, and fighting back just fuels the fire of self-righteousness that bullies like Dita use as their excuse.

But there is no excuse for bullying. If you abuse others, you're just an arsehole that spits a lot of shit all over everyone, including yourself. The fact that you don't see it or smell it doesn't mean that it isn't there, and one day, it will make you sick.

Dita, however, is as tenacious as the dog in his gravatar would be if he got his teeth clamped around a piece of tasty flesh. He's managed to keep the whole thing going well past its natural use-by date.

My anger flares, and though the raw energy of it is highly appropriate for the weather, if I hold onto it, it will become the rope that hangs me. I can't stop him from doing what he wants, but I can stop him from taking away my calm.

With a switch of perspective, I transform the smouldering embers of my anger into a blaze of compassion.

Dita has failed. Though he most likely doesn't know it, his abuse has backfired.

The dog tried to spread his shit over me, but I ducked every bit he threw. It stuck to his paws, and every time he scratched himself, he smeared it all over his wiry coat. Every time he licked himself, he ate his own shit. It's so old now that it has dried and stuck to his hair. I expect it itches, but tongue lashings and claw scratching don't get it off. Nothing other than a full immersion in clean soapy water will remove it now, but he has no owner to take care of him, and bits of shit fall into his mouth with every bite he takes.

37

In the Gaze of the Buddha

The thunder ceases but the roar of the water rushing down the stream bed is so loud that rocks and trees are probably rolling down it. I'd love to take a look, but it's too dangerous. I shine the torch out the back door on my return to the living room though, and find water where there shouldn't be any. A blocked drain! Great. They're only ever blocked when you need them.

Who choreographed this damn dance? Oh, yeah, that's right; it's improvised, and therefore dangerous because you never know how it will turn out.

I grab an umbrella and open the door to the car port. Merlin races through my legs and runs outside. Damn cat. I do not need to be chasing him in this weather. But I know he won't go far. A flash of the torch reveals him sitting and staring at the water rising rapidly onto the concrete. Leave it too long and it will be lapping at the back door. I scoop him up, drop him inside and close the door in his indignant face.

Clearing the drain would be fine if the outside light worked, but with an umbrella in one hand and a torch in the other, it's practically impossible. The torch

I need, but the umbrella has alternatives. I can don full wet-weather gear, or strip off. It's not cold, so I strip off and dive into the rain stark naked. Cold water pounds on my scalp and shoulders, soaks my hair in an instant and dribbles down my face and over my breasts. I throw up my arms, turn my face to the sky and spin around, giggling like some mad woman. The storm consumes me, and I love the energy of it. But it's not that warm, and I don't want to be here long enough to get chilled.

The water is up to my calves already and is too murky for the torch to shine through, so I have to feel around for the drain. My hand scrabbles over rough concrete and finds a clump of leaves and dirt—that's it—I scoop the debris out with one hand and deposit it on the grass. The water begins to drain. Three scoops later, my fingers feel the grate. I yank it off and feel the finer muck beneath it. That's the real cause of the problem; it blocks the flow of the water just as Dita and Scott interrupt the flow of my life. If I scoop it onto the grass, it will just wash down and block the drain again. I need a more permanent solution, so I grab a bucket from the woodshed and fill it with the muck, then I whip the grate back on and leap under the car port. Water flowing down a drain is a beautiful sight, especially when it wasn't flowing a moment ago.

I wish my life would get back to its usual free-flowing state. I sigh and look at the muck. It will be good on the garden. 'Instead of being a nuisance, you can make the roses bloom', I say to no one.

Then it hits me: I can see Dita and Scott as shit, or as fertiliser. They're stinky and sticky, but instead of trying to get rid of them, I can use them to make this rose bloom. The revelation is so obvious that I kick myself for not seeing it before. It's called taking obstacles as the path. Everything can be used as fuel to fire your journey to enlightenment. They're giving me the perfect opportunity to grow. The possibility of actually feeling gratitude to my tormentors glimmers in my awareness.

A shiver reminds me that I'm naked. I need to get warm.

Only as I grab my clothes and head to the door do I remember Scott's unscheduled visit, and I suddenly feel vulnerable and slightly stupid. I flick my torch from shrubs to shed to garden enclosure and back again, squinting into darkness between lightning flashes. I console myself that no person in their right mind would be wandering around in this—especially not naked! That sends me into a fit of giggles, until I consider the possibility that Scott may not be in his right mind.

Back inside, I wrap my dressing gown around me and a towel around my head, then grab the meditation cushion I keep under the coffee table, sit on it with my legs crossed and stare through the lounge room windows into the storm.

May all beings have happiness and the causes of happiness.

I think of Dita as I say the prayer. Truly, may he be released from his torment. He has to do it himself, of course, but I hope my prayer will help. At least it helps me. Compassion is a great deal healthier than anger.

I send my love and compassion, set ablaze by the heartfelt prayer, to him and to all those who suffer, and the power of it holds the whole universe in its embrace. My mind is the universe, vast, brilliant and never ending. And I realise how quickly I can arrive at this state now—no matter what the circumstances I find myself in. I've had a lot of practise recently.

Dita has failed. His abuse has only made me stronger.

I smile. The forest before me, flashing silver in the darkness, becomes an ornate shrine. I am transported back to the temple in the south of France. Once again, as I did for three long years, I sit before the huge golden Buddha. The crown of his head almost touches the glass roof two stories above me, and smaller statues, but no less glorious, flank him on either side. My vajra brothers and sisters surround me, all of us sitting in the calm, compassionate gaze of the Buddha.

This memory, deeply engraved in my heart and mind through days of teachings and meditation practice, is my rock in the stormy seas of my life. Evoking and re-experiencing it calms the ocean, and I remember that, whether calm or peaking in furious waves, it is all the same water. Now it is so calm and clear that I can see into the depths.

I have nothing to fear. With a mind like this, I can handle anything.

Thank you, Dita, for pushing me to practise. You'd kick yourself if you knew how much you've helped me.

38

Hack

Morning comes still without power. I edit until the battery dies on my laptop, then I sit on the veranda in the warm morning and stare at the waterfall in the front garden. The unfinished edit could weigh on me if I let it, but there's nothing I can do about it, so why waste the energy. I take a holiday instead. No electricity brings freedom of a kind.

The water trickles down the rock with a cheerful song, and Merlin rubs against my calves, purring loudly. Morning birds chatter and flitter about us. I'm glad I keep Merlin on a leash. I've seen the feral glint in his eyes. He's a mean, cream killing machine for birds and lizards. It's his nature.

I wish I could set him on Dita.

I giggle and turn my awareness onto the feral thought. It skitters away as if it knows its own irrelevance in the world beneath the veil.

I keep my attention on the waterfall. The splash of its fall makes ripples in the pond. They roll across the surface and dissolve back into the water just before they reach the other side, disappearing as thoughts do when you leave them alone.

A bird flies past too close. Merlin can't help himself. It's natural to him. A run and a leap later and he has the bird, squawking in panic now, in his mouth.

'Drop it,' I say and race towards him. He growls and keeps his mouth tight around the bird struggling in his jaws. I distract him enough for him to relax his grip and the bird, a lovely little finch, flies free.

Merlin runs to the end of his leash and strains against it, watching the bird fly away.

'Sorry, Merlin, but you're not a natural part of this ecosystem. The balance here is weighted in your favour.' He just looks pissed off.

Would I let him off the leash if that was Dita? Wanting to is as natural for me as chasing a bird is to Merlin, but I don't live in a cave where I have to fight predators to stay alive. The world doesn't work that way anymore, and though the primitive part of my brain wants to fight, there are more skilful ways.

Let the bastard shout in a vacuum.

Another giggle. I don't believe my own vehemence, so the thought ripple naturally dissolves back into the water of my mind.

The kitchen light flashes on behind me. I sigh. The power's on again. Time to go to work.

I grab the cat, unclip the leash from his harness and carry him inside. As soon as I've released him from his harness, he's off, galloping from one end of the house to the other, his paws thumping on the wooden floors.

I turn on my laptop and modem and prepare for another good editing stint. I've not been at it long when a ding tells me someone has messaged me. It's Liz.

Either you've done a complete turnabout or you've been hacked. Check your blog.

Hacked. Shit. Is she serious?

I remember Dita's words from last night.

Take it down or I'll take you down.

I bet he thought that was poetic.

I click the bookmark for my blog, and take the time while it loads to shield my mind against the attack. I'm surprisingly calm, but this is, after all, just another opportunity to practice sticking on the right side of the veil. Someone has broken into my online home. I should feel violated, and in some part of my being I do, but it doesn't bother me; my mind is too strong this morning. I do wonder what has been stolen, and the thought makes me smile. Pixels is all an online robber can steal—unless he's hacked my bank account too— just bits of electricity making a pattern from circuits turning on and off.

And my reputation. Online robbers who steal people's reputations are called bullies; but reputation is nothing. We think it's so terribly important, but it isn't tangible. An attack on your reputation isn't like an attack on your body. Sure, it can affect your livelihood, but the only kind of pain it can inflict is the mental kind, the kind we have control over.

His punch will not land on me.

Let his fist fly into empty space and drag him stumbling after it. Let him fall from the momentum he started. I think this with compassion, not vehemence, because karma will surely make it happen sooner or later.

The words on my blog form, and I read.

Apparently, I've had some kind of realisation— or a rearrangement of my brain. It seems that the nature of top quality books has nothing to do with grammar, punctuation or elegant prose and everything to do with spontaneity. And the 'new best books' are not defined by the old rules regarding character development, plot, pacing and so on. Anything goes and everything is good. I think the author is trying to have me say that I've been narrow minded and vindictive, but I'm not quite sure, because the language isn't clear. I press my lips together and shake my head. It's obviously Dita. The post is as badly worded as the guy's book. My regular readers couldn't possibly think I wrote that. Could they?

Reading his writing is like watching an un-trained dancer trying to dance a ballet. He believes that anyone can ballet dance, and is so deluded that he actually thinks he's doing it beautifully. All the rest of us see is someone flailing around. It's embarrassing to watch. His friends are in the back row cheering away though. Would they see the difference even if I put Baryshnikov on stage beside him?

I've already inoculated my mind against the threat, so though my heart does pound a little harder and my teeth clench, I simply note the irritation—it's natural—and let it fade of its own accord. It won't hang around to bug me unless I keep thinking about what caused it in the first place. That would be like picking at a scab. No, I'm not stupid.

Damage control is all that's required now, angst is optional, and I'm not buying. I simply have to take a series of steps to regain control of my website, then fix the damage. I refuse to let Dita take more time away from my editing job, so I resist the urge to go in the back end of the site, but it's a struggle, and a wave of anger washes over me.

Don't let this eat you up from the inside.

I watch the anger and let it pass unhindered. It dissolves harmlessly, and a flush of energy surges in its wake. I silently thank my lama for teaching me how to survive my emotions. And I congratulate myself on my discipline. Self-righteousness makes anger very enticing. The desire to indulge is strong. It might be fun to roll around in the mud for a while, but you still end up dirty, and the more mud you get on you, the harder it is to get out of the mire.

Meditating after an attack is getting to be a habit now, but it's a good one. Though on the surface it drives me crazy each time he attacks, some part of me gains a degree of satisfaction in the knowledge that my ability to clear my mind quickly is growing stronger.

I guess Dita has no one to help him handle his feelings. Or perhaps he does, but he's so covered in mud that he can't get a grip on any hand that offers to help. I see him sliding down a muddy bank, filthy hands reaching up but grabbing only air. He splashes into thick mud at the bottom and sinks beneath the surface. A moment later, his head reappears, gasping for breath. Mud covers his eyes. It's all he can see. *There, but for the grace of my meditation teacher and my own discipline, go I.*

I really do feel sorry for the guy. I pray that he finds someone to help him climb out of the muddy pool of his anger.

Luckily, my web designer is online and replies to my message almost immediately. He assures me that he'll get it all under control and will take the site offline until it's secure again.

Time to move on. I'm going to get some work done.

No, wait. I go to Facebook and thank Liz—it really helped to have advance warning. Then I post an update to let everyone know I've been hacked. I shoot the message out on Twitter as well, not that anyone is likely to actually read it there, but I've notified the world of my social networks, and told them that I'm working on the problem. It will all be solved soon and this event, like all others, will fade into the past.

Unless I keep thinking about it. Which I swear I will not do.

Until I notice another of Dita's hate-Ella tweets in my mentions column. How sick is someone who adds @EllaSmith to a tweet that abuses me! I honestly think he does more damage to himself than to me. That @ tells everyone that he's trying to upset me. Charming fellow.

I've had enough.

Ignoring it works for me because I don't find it too difficult to stay off that particular form of social media, but I'm pretty sure there are other things I can do as well. I google what to do when you're being bullied on Twitter and discover that Dita's tweets fit the 'use of hate speech, making threats and defamation' categories. With a sigh of resignation, I follow the suggested steps. I block him first—it won't stop him, but I won't have to look at it—and I report him to Twitter. I'm supposed to keep copies of everything, but doing that will take even more time than the bastard has already stolen from me, and I'd have to read them all, something I'd rather not do.

I think about all my friends on social media, the real friends who cheer me on, commiserate with me and tell me the truth. I'm grateful for those friends, but they can't hold my hand or give me a cuddle, and right now, I could really do with one. The idea of having a partner is suddenly quite appealing.

39

Email from the Author

Hi Ella

I thought about it and I agree that a lot of readers won't like it, but it will make an impact and that's what I'm aiming for. If Slade lives, Kelee goes to Sheldra with him, and the reason is because his brother said it was the one place where her father wouldn't look for her. That's a pretty lame reason. Without Slade, she makes the decision to go herself, and for much stronger reasons; reasons that emerge from her reaction to his death. I want her to face the trials in the rest of the book alone and to triumph herself, not as part of a duo.

His death changes her; it makes her stronger, more self-reliant. I think it's important that our female characters are strong role models. Slade's death is her trial by fire, and she must go through it to change her priorities from an infatuated teen to a self-reliant woman.

Please continue editing the book as it is.

BTW the possibility of a future romance appears at the end of the book.

Thanks

Tanya Khan.

Disappointment washes over me. I'm amazed at how much I want Slade to live and how wrong I think her decision is. If she'd decided to change it, I'd get more time for the job too. But she's the author; what she says goes. I get back to work, but find little pleasure in Kelee's World without Slade in it.

40

Stalker

I'm sitting on the couch with my computer on my lap. It's late. I should be in bed, but I just want to finish editing this chapter.

Merlin growls.

I've never heard him growl before.

I look up from my laptop and stare at him in amazement. He was asleep a moment ago, but now he's sitting up in his bed by the hearth staring at the window. The hair on his back rises like a Mohawk hairstyle, and he stalks towards the window, staying low.

What the ...? It's too dark to see anything. I wonder what he's sensed.

Merlin growls again, low and mean. He's under the coffee table. I bend down to take a look. He's not moving. His eyes are wide and fixed on the window. I swallow, but my throat is suddenly dry. What, or who, is out there?

Have I got a stalker?

Duh!

My heart pounds, and I take a deep breath to ease away the tension. The doors are all locked—I've been diligent since Scott's visit—but my old-fashioned locks are woefully inadequate if anyone really wanted to get in, and by the time the police arrived here, I could be dead. I feel suddenly exposed. Someone is out there watching me. I can feel it. His eyes are like laser beams burning into my skin.

Scott? Would he?

I stand and yank the curtains across the window. Merlin slips through the crack between them. I peek through. He's crouched beneath the low sill, his ears flat against his skull, wide eyes fixed on the night. I shiver and close the crack. Whatever's out there, Merlin's animal instinct is telling him it's not good.

I listen. Silence. Even the frogs aren't singing tonight. I perch on the edge of the couch, wondering what to do. My senses are highly alert, and my mind is bright. I wait, like a cat waiting for prey.

A twig snaps in the garden. Is there someone out there? Or is it just my imagination? I'm not about to go outside to find out. I decide to hide—just in case. It's time for bed anyway. I get up, grab my torch from the charger, flick off the room light and, leaving the torch turned off, creep into my bedroom in the dark. The curtains are already closed, but I'm not getting into my PJs. I do consider changing my fluffy ugg boots for my studded demon kickers— if Scott's out there, he really does need his butt kicked—but I'm not half as tough as I'd like to be.

Torch in hand, I slide beneath my feather doona fully clothed and lie on my back, listening. Can

I hear footsteps, or is it just a wombat rustling through the shrubs? Whatever. Tomorrow, I'm calling a locksmith.

Merlin growls from the bottom of the French doors. Someone is just outside. I can feel it. And it has to be Scott. Who else could it be? My breathing's too fast. I consciously take deeper, slower breaths. My heart slows, then speeds up abruptly when the door rattles a little.

My thumb automatically flicks on the torch. I shine the beam on the door knob. It turns slowly then back again as the person outside tests to see if it's locked. I flick off the torch, pull my arm back beneath the covers and wait.

I hear it turn again.

The online stalking pales into insignificance against this! My heart is yammering against my ribcage, and I'm so scared, I can barely breathe. But my mind remains relatively calm—considering. I guess I can thank Dita for the practice.

Merlin growls again. He never growls, not even when he faced off that snake, but I get the sense that he's protecting me. I imagine him leaping on Scott and gouging his eyes out.

The stalker creeps away. I'm so attuned to the night now that I can hear every footfall. He's walking behind the bedroom. I expect he'll check all the doors. I did lock them all, didn't I? I reassure myself by recalling myself locking every one. Yes. I'm safe. So long as he can't get in.

This is real. Horribly real, not merely pixels on a screen. I let the fear wash through me. I will not succumb to its crippling embrace.

I want to cuddle Merlin, but I hear his feet pad softly through the door. It sounds like he's going to follow the stalker. I'm staying here, trusting that the locks will keep him out.

I need a distraction, so I turn to my phone. Notifications tell me that I have a message on Facebook. It's Liz.

He's at it again

Who? I think I know, but she could be talking about her errant son.

That author

Dita?

Yeah, him. Cathy told me she came across him on a forum. I took a look. He's attacking your editing ability now

Damn. Is that why I haven't had any new clients? This could hurt my finances. *Did you say anything?*

I listed a couple of the books you edited & said people could read them to see the quality. Also said Dita had been bullying you over an honest review

How did that go down?

One author said she'd read abuse from him before, so she dismissed his comment as personal vendetta

Awesome. And?

A couple of comments against author bullying. One said he should be removed from the forum. His next comments showed up as deleted by the moderator. Then they closed the thread

It helps when moderators are on the ball

Yeah, they gagged him. Pity more don't do it

Thanks for the support

No worries. Are you coming to Sydney with me next week?

Merlin races past the door. Dita and Scott merge into one. They're both out there. Hounding me. I rejected them both. Seems some men are just a tad too sensitive. They should stay home with their mummy and leave the big world to the big kids.

Ella. You ok?

Yeah. No. Someone is walking around outside

What? Who?

Scott? Maybe

Can you see him?

No, but …

Call the cops

2 late. I locked the doors. He'll go away eventually

What if he breaks in?

Not helping!

Sorry

It's ok. I listened. Nothing. At least nothing I could hear for the moment. *I think he's gone*

Thank God

I'm going to sleep now

You sure you're okay?

Yeah fine. Goodnight

Okay. C ya.

I am okay, just as long as he can't get into the house, and I am not going to let this guy bother me. I visualise a white rose and rest my mind on the image. No matter what rises, I simply keep looking at the rose, just looking, not commenting. Thoughts and feelings rise and fall away, and my mind soon returns to its calm. My ability to clear my mind quickly is growing stronger.

I doze in and out of sleep, wondering if he really is gone. A twisted hybrid of Dita and Scott stalks the ever-dusky forest of my dreams. The shadowy beast carries a huge gun slung low at his crotch. Or is it a penis? I can't tell exactly. In true dream fashion, it's probably both. This hulking symbol of the men who stalk me creeps around like a soldier looking for enemies. I hide, then sneak away when the beast is looking elsewhere. I find a cave and cower inside. But I wish I didn't have to cower. I wish I could race out and slaughter the beast.

Every now and then, I jolt awake, my heart racing at some sound—real or imagined, I don't know. I bring a golden Buddha to mind and focus on that to stop my mind spinning stories to feed my fear. Eventually, I calm down again and doze off.

At some point, Merlin jumps onto the bed and snuggles down beside me. Only then do I put my PJs on and roll onto my side. It's three AM and the forest feels right again. I breathe more easily.

My mind shelves the problem until tomorrow, but it doesn't completely calm the seed of anger that simmers in my gut.

I'm buying a baseball bat tomorrow.

41

Battle

My fingers wrap around the hilt of my sword. I grasp it firmly and draw it without a sound as the footsteps creep closer. I wait in readiness, unmoving with my back hard against the tree. Since when did breathing sound so loud?

Snap.

My heart jumps. I press my lips together and breathe in slowly—and far too lightly, but I cannot risk him hearing me. I do not move. He is close now. I'm counting on the element of surprise.

Crack.

My eyes fly wide. My muscles coil ready to spring.

Rustle.

I jump from my hiding place and thrust my blade at the hulking, faceless beast. He grows, and though he makes no words, I understand his anger. I have rejected him.

'No,' I tell him as he parries my blow with his crude weapon—an ugly, rusted blade. 'I merely tell the truth.' He swipes. I parry and deliver an upwards cut before he can attack again. He's heavier and larger than me, but he moves slower as well.

He grunts and jumps away from my blade. A burble of sound emerges from the beast. Anger burns in his eyes and fuels a brutal attack that reduces me to mere defence. Metal clangs against metal, the sound chilling in the quiet forest. The animals and birds have become silent. He pushes me back, step by step. I manage to avoid getting stuck with my back against a tree, but his blows are too heavy.

I muster my strength and fight back. I use my speed and duck around him. My cuts and thrusts are so fast that I put him on the defensive. His half-formed features twist and he spits a stream of vivid red fire. I cannot keep this up. The strength of his blows have weakened me.

'Leave me alone,' I say. 'I only fight because you fight me.' But who will stop first? Not him, for sure. I am sick of running and hiding. I feint, aiming high. He blocks high. I drop to the ground, roll towards him and thrust my sword into his belly.

His screech needs no translation. He staggers back, trips over a stone and falls, hitting the ground with a thud like a felled tree. His sword drops from his hand, bounces off a rock and lays still. I stand over him; his blood drips from my sword, but I feel no satisfaction. Nor do I feel remorse.

His features shift, as if trying to form. I gasp and step back as his furry hide transforms into skin, his torso becomes slender and more human, and his face takes on Scott's visage. I gulp. Have I murdered him? I see myself swinging from gallows.

He clutches his stomach and curses me, very much alive. I'm not sure whether to be relieved or annoyed. 'Cock teaser!' he spits out. 'You owe me.'

My jaw drops. I only went to dinner with him, and I'm sure I said and did nothing suggestive. I didn't even wear anything too sexy. Though perhaps I showed a little cleavage. Surely, he didn't take that as a come-on?

I shake my head in disbelief and look around for an alternative. I must eject this man from my life, but how? I can't kill him when he isn't attacking. Perhaps he'll die if I just walk away.

A lyre bird calls, crisp, clear and sharp. It's mimicking the blades clashing. The battle has changed this forest. Will I ever feel safe here again?

I turn to walk away, sensing that this is just a bad dream, but I hear Scott stagger to his feet behind me. No; I will not cower in fear of this man again. I spin back just as he leaps forward, a shiny, sharp sword in his hand. I jump aside and swing my sword in an arc towards his neck. He wavers from his injury and fails to block.

His head rolls to the ground. His body slumps like a puppet with its strings cut.

This time, I feel satisfaction.

I wake with a smile on my face and determination in my heart.

42

The Yogi

The snow has receded enough for me to open the door built across the entrance to the cave. I step outside, and though the sky is clear, I know immediately that something is wrong. It is as if the whole valley holds its breath.

A sharp sound cuts the still mountain air with shocking violence. A hunter? No; hunters need only one shot, at the most two, and today the gunfire continues. Countless shots, all running together and from an impossible direction—the village. Who can afford to waste ammunition, and what are they shooting at down there?

I smell it before I see it, and my body tenses. Something inside me knows already what this day will bring.

I step to the edge of my mountain realm and gaze once more at the familiar view. Far in the distance, smoke curls into the sky from a mighty blaze. The monastery is burning. I am already too late to stop the flames. It will take me half a day to reach the village, but I must go. I pray there will be survivors I can help.

I pause before returning to the cave to gather some things. I feel I will have no need of them anyway. All of Tibet burns today.

Hours later, I draw close to the village and see that more than just the monastery burns. The cries of survivors wrench my heart, but I take the back route and head straight for the monastery. The books. The statues. The tangkhas. Has Rinpoche escaped? Is there any hope? My heart beats painfully. The whole world will be diminished if our teachings are lost.

And lost they are. No book could survive the ruin.

I draw to a stop in the courtyard, tears trickling down my face. The flames are finished, the door a gaping maw, the beautiful painted wood turned to dust. Just a few heavy wooden beams smoulder amongst the crumbling blackened walls. The carnage is worse than I could ever have imagined. Dozens of monks, my students, my friends and my teachers, lie in pools of blood, shot as they fled the blaze. Some were not running. They lie crumpled where they stood. Some are missing ears, one lacks a nose—hacked from his living face by some barbarian; blood obscures his features, saving me from the pain of knowing his identity. My stomach heaves, though I have nothing but bile to offer.

How could anyone do this? No monk carries a gun, or even wields a stick in anger. Our vows forbid harming sentient beings. Clearly the perpetrators do not realise how many eons they will suffer in the hot and cold hells for this. I pray for the perpetrators as well as the victims, but still I feel my anger rise, and it is only with great difficulty that I let it pass.

I search for Rinpoche amongst the bodies, praying that he, at least, has escaped, but I can hardly see through my tears, and my breath comes in painful cinder-filled gasps. Fear-filled faces stare up at me through dead eyes. I close them as I go and scatter mantras like rose petals over the corpses.

Blood and ashes stain my boots. But this horrible deed stains all of China, and one day they will pay a price for this ignorance. The thought brings me no solace.

The ground has fallen away from beneath my feet, leaving just the great impermanence. I have helped many through the bardos, but never faced the truth of impermanence on such a scale. The shock is indescribable. No one should ever have to face this kind of thing, and these gentle souls, of all people and no matter what their karma, did not deserve this violent death.

Tashi's old mother hobbles towards me. Her eyes are red, a great sadness etched into the lines of her face. She tugs on my sleeve. 'Come away,' she whispers hoarsely. 'They are still about. I have hidden some of the relics. We must wait until they are well away.'

'Rinpoche?' I manage to croak.

She shakes her head.

'No!' I shout before I have a chance to stifle the sound. Anger burns through me at the injustice.

Crack!

The old woman falls at my feet.

Crack!

Pain explodes in my back and consumes me. My legs refuse to hold me up. I fall, twisting to face my murderers. They walk on without a glance.

I pray that the teachings will survive and take root elsewhere. Countless beings need them. These men most of all.

I die with my lama's face in my mind. Though it is bloodied and bruised, there is no fear, neither in his eyes nor in my heart.

I come back to myself with a start. I'm sitting in my meditation hut in some kind of waking dream. Is this real? I wonder. The mental clarity is real. If I write it down, we'd call it fiction because it sprang from my mind, but how did it come there? It could have happened, and even if it isn't a past life remembered, somewhere this happened to someone.

Chinese troops in Tibet did cut off monks' ears and noses, and gouged out their eyes and tongues. The cruelty and the systematic destruction of this ancient wisdom culture breaks my heart, as does all the iniquity, and all the pain and suffering inflicted on mankind by mankind. My stalker is nothing compared to the reality of others' lives. The thought brings me no solace, but does put my own small concerns into perspective.

One thing's for sure though. I'm not going to let anyone come in here and destroy my life. I'm going to fight. And the first step is getting in a good few hours' work on my editing job.

43

Arming Up

My fingers tighten around the grip on the baseball bat. I pull it back over my shoulder, then swing it around— hard. I imagine the crack it might make as it hits a skull.

'Looks like you're trying to knock someone's head off,' the smiling sports' shop assistant says. He thinks it's a joke.

'Yeah. My little brother's.'

The guy's eyebrows shoot up and his mouth drops down. His tanned face and sun-bleached straggly hair mark him as a surfer.

'Joking,' I say. He releases his breath, visibly relieved, and I hope the police aren't ever going to have to investigate me over killing someone with a baseball bat. If I don't hit hard enough, I probably won't knock him out, but if I hit too hard … 'Actually, it's for my little brother.'

'Right.' He's smiling now.

'I'll take it, thanks.' I hand him the bat, and he walks towards the cash register with a smile. I have no intention of actually hitting anyone with the thing—

unless they break into my house, and I'm about to make that a lot more difficult.

The locksmith's shop in Nowra, about the size of my kitchen, has a counter on one side with shelves full of little boxes behind it. One display stand in the corner opposite the counter explains the different locks and their purposes. I shake my head and look at the list in my hand where I have diligently noted every door and window in my house. This is going to cost a packet!

'Can I help you?' a rich male voice asks from behind me.

My heart jumps. I hear the remains of an English accent. I turn, and I can't stop the grin spreading across my face. It's the mystery man from the market! 'Hi,' I say.

Brown eyes crinkling at the corners fix on me with a twinkle. 'We met at the market, right?'

I nod, still grinning. I can't believe my luck—and I'm sorely in need of some luck right now.

'You sold me a mask I didn't want.'

'You didn't want it?'

'Not until I saw who was selling it.' The corners of his full mouth curl and one eyebrow raises a challenge.

'Um, right.' Yeah, I do a verbal stumble, but, hey, I'm here to turn my home into a fortress, not flirt with some ex-pat Englishman, and I can't quite get my head around what's happening.

'Don't get me wrong, I love it; I just wasn't planning on getting anything for myself.' He pauses, tilts his head slightly and stares right into my eyes before continuing. 'Mind you, I didn't get what I really wanted.'

His smile sends a tingle through my body. 'And what was that?'

'Your phone number.'

I stifle a gasp. 'Do you flirt with all the girls who come in here?'

'Nah, not girls, only women, and only if they have blue hair, no wedding ring and look like they could hold an intelligent conversation.'

My jaw drops at his openness.

His chuckle turns to a full laugh.

'What? You don't think that was pretty forward?'

'It was, but what's life without a little risk-taking?' He fixes his eyes on mine, and I know why he's set aside any reserves he might normally have; he's determined not to miss another opportunity to … get my number. I smile. I'm totally with him on that.

'Yeah, well … I need to lower the risks in my life, which is why I'm here. Someone's been roaming around outside at night, and I don't want them getting in. I need someone to take a look and give me a quote on what I need to make the house properly secure.'

His eyes widen. 'You have a stalker?'

I grimace. I hadn't meant to mention that. 'I guess I do.' Two of them, actually.

'You told the police?' Concern furrows his brow and laces his voice with honey.

I shake my head. 'It's not like they'll do a stake-out and catch him, is it?'

He considers that for a moment, then nods. 'Where do you live?'

I catch his eye.

'Risk assessment,' he assures me. 'Professional reasons only.'

'Rose Valley.'

'How far up?'

'Near the top.'

He shakes his head, and I can tell his concern is real. 'You have to tell the police. Even if they can't do anything, they need to know. There're no lights up there, no people for miles. Anyone live with you? A boyfriend, perhaps?'

The twinkle is back in his eyes. I chuckle now and he joins me. I've just admitted that the interest is mutual. 'No boyfriend.'

He leans against the counter, tilts his head and regards me with a measured look. 'You interested in fixing that?'

'I'm interested in turning my house into Fort Knox.'

He grins again. 'Then you've come to the right place. How about I come up and take a look?'

'Do you charge for house calls?'

'Not for you.'

I roll my eyes. 'When can you come?'

He whistles slowly. 'Whenever you want, ma'am, whenever you want.'

Right now, I want to hit him. The suggestion in his tone was unmistakable.

His expression turns sheepish. 'Sorry, that was uncalled for. I've probably just shot myself in the foot.'

Now it's my turn to tilt my head, narrow my eyes and give an appraising look. 'Let's see how big your quote is.' Both our jaws drop at the same time and we burst out laughing. 'I can't believe I said that,' I say between gasps.

He shakes his head and presses his lips together, trying to bring his laughter under control, but just when it seems we might be able to continue the conversation, he chuckles again and fights to rein it in. Something good must be coming. He finally schools his expression, then blurts out, 'I'll keep it small, I promise.' He cracks up again, and I shake with giggles. The man's laugh is infectious.

Eventually, the giggles subside. I wipe my eyes but can't keep the grin off my face. I haven't laughed so much for a long time, and it feels good—really good.

He clears his throat, grabs a pad and pen and pushes them across the counter towards me—all back to business. 'Name, address and phone number, please.'

I shoot him a smile and wonder what his hair would feel like in my fingers, then I can't believe I'm thinking that.

He watches in silence as I write, and I'm very aware of his proximity on the other side of the counter. There's an electric current flowing between us. I think our pheromones are hooking up.

'Ella? That's nice,' he says when I hand the paper back. 'My name's Jamie.' He extends a hand across the counter. I shake it. It's cool and pleasantly firm. I imagine him raising my hand to his lips, but he doesn't, of course.

I give him directions and we agree on a time. I have a couple of hours to get home and tidy the place up. Our interaction is subdued, business-like, but the undercurrent is of two people who've shared something intimate.

'I'm not like that with everyone,' he says when we finish the business. 'I hope you didn't think me inappropriate; my apologies if you did.'

Our eyes meet. His smile is genuine, as are his words. I believe him. 'Do I look offended?'

He shakes his head. 'Just thought I should check.'

'Probably wise, but no, it's all good. I enjoyed the banter.'

'Great. I'll see you later, then.' His eyes hold both a question and a promise.

I smile. 'I look forward to it.'

I've answered his question.

44

Jamie

The fire—set low and with Merlin curled up on the mat in front of it—hums in the living room and casts a soft glow through my bedroom door. The curtains are closed, and I'm sitting on my bed, propped against the wall with pillows at my back. I have glimpses of stillness between gentle thoughts and pleasant memories of Jamie's assessment of my security.

I've discovered that he is, actually, a great guy. His behaviour as he checked my locks confirmed my initial impressions. He remained totally professional as he walked around and looked at all the doors and windows, and asked me questions about the degree of armour I wanted and the limit of my budget. But at the same time, he managed to gently extract all the pertinent information about me by noting various things:

My cake mixer: yes, I like to bake.

My office desk; yes, work at home.

My overflowing bookshelves, yes, I like to read. That's when I found out, to my great delight, that he was a reader. Not just someone who read occasionally, but one of those people who always had a book to read.

No wonder he had a good vocabulary. This boded well for intelligent conversations and lots of topics of interest—exactly what I hadn't found in Scott.

My photo wall: yes, I was a ballet dancer, and I have no brothers or sisters. The usual family questions followed naturally, and my framed degree needed no explanation.

My shrine room; yes, I'm a Buddhist in the Tibetan tradition—that one was easy. I don't normally let people see that, but he needed to see all the windows.

And so on; you get the idea.

I used his questions to bat some of my own back at him on the same topics, and by the time we sat down for a cup of tea and to work out a plan, we knew as much about each other as you would on a first date. He'd lived in Australia for the last twenty years, which explained the subservience of his English accent, and he'd come out at the age of eighteen with his childhood sweetheart to escape his parents' displeasure at his choice of mate. His father had since passed on, but the rest of his family—his mother, older brother and younger sister—still lived in England. The girl he'd left England with had become his wife, but she died in a car accident three years ago, and he hadn't dated since.

'It took me a long time to get over her death,' he told me while staring into the garden. 'In fact, get over it is the wrong phrase. I don't think I'll ever be over it, but I've accepted it, and I'm ready to move on with my life.' He turned to me and smiled. 'I might even consider asking someone out to dinner. It would make my mother very happy; she's been trying to hook me up ever since …' He shrugged. 'Are you interested?'

'Are you asking me out?'

He nodded. 'I really enjoy your company.' The vulnerability in his eyes made him look like a little boy.

My heart had already warmed towards him, but now I simply couldn't refuse. The truth of those simple words washed my reticence away like swift-flowing water flushing sediment from a mountain stream.

'Sure, I'll come. I'd like to make your mother happy.'

He grinned. Forget about his mother, his expression told me, I'd already made him happy. And I felt lighter than I had for far too long. I couldn't help thinking how the stalking with all its associated anxiety and inconvenience had a positive side; it had led me to this delightful man. If Jamie turned out to be the love of my life, I might even be able to think of Scott in a positive way.

I mentally cut through the hope that bubbled in my chest; fear always followed in its wake—fear that he wouldn't be the one, that no one ever would be. Damn it, I'm perfectly happy alone.

We decided to forget about keyed locks on all the windows—my budget simply didn't stretch that far—and concentrate on turning the old door locks into something harder to pick or smash through. I made a cup of tea and laid out some home-made cookies while he sat at the dining room table, pressed buttons on a calculator and scribbled on a piece of paper. He handed it over. I glanced at the price and said it was all fine. He said he'd be back tomorrow to fit the locks. Then I noticed the name on the top of the paper:

'James Claypole!' I couldn't help chuckling. 'Claypole is your surname.'

He winced and shook his head. 'Unfortunately, yes … and it's not that funny.'

'Sorry, it's not … it's just … I know how you feel; my name is actually Prunella. So we have Prunella Smith and James Claypole.'

Now he chuckled. 'Prunella! My God, that's a real doozy.'

'Yeah, my mum wanted something unusual to make up for the Smith bit.'

'At least it shortens nicely.'

'That's what my father said.' I stifled a giggle at the thought of being called Prunella Claypole then vowed not to think further on that matter.

The conversation turned to the stalker. 'Any idea who it is?' Jamie asked after we'd covered the basic facts of when, where and what exactly.

I nodded. No point hiding it, only someone who knew me would come all the way up here to creep me out. 'I'm pretty sure it's a guy I went to dinner with a couple of weeks ago, but I have no proof. I didn't actually see him.' Jamie grew visibly uneasy as I filled him in on the story, and he grimaced when I said that Scott felt I owed him something.

'The guy's dangerous,' he said in a voice that was far too serious for my liking.

'You're making me feel worse.'

'Sorry; it's just … you're so … alone up here.'

'I'm fine.' I refilled my tea cup and offered him another cookie.

He shook his head. 'Do you have someone who could stay here with you tonight? I could if you wanted—on the couch, of course.'

I smile. I know he's not suggesting anything else, but I don't want to tempt fate in that area just yet. 'I don't think it's necessary. Surely, he's unlikely to come back two nights in a row.'

Jamie shrugs. 'Who knows; but I'll sleep easier tonight if I knew someone else was up here with you. That back door could be opened far too easily.'

A wave of anxiety washed over me, tensing my muscles. I slipped into the bedroom and came back with the baseball bat. 'I have a contingency plan.'

His jaw dropped. 'You're not serious!'

'Deadly so. If he dares set a foot in my house, he'll wake up with a huge headache.'

That boyish grin came back.

I chuckled.

'I guess I'd better go before I outstay my welcome and you use that thing on me.'

I rested it on the table. 'I know where you work.'

When Jamie left, I spent the rest of the day working on Kelee's story—I didn't go near any social media, just in case Dita wanted to try some other way to sabotage my work. That and the excitement—I only reluctantly admit that word fits—of meeting Jamie pushed thoughts of anything else clean out of my head.

I did consider staying the night with Liz, but not seriously. I'm not fond of the noise in her house, and I'd be stuck on a blow-up mattress in their family room. Besides, I see no reason why Scott would come back at all. It's not like I'm ever going to invite him in. I cut through the next thought before it has a chance to finish forming, but I know the end of it anyway—maybe he isn't planning on waiting for an invitation.

It's too late now, anyway. The only place I'm going tonight is bed. I have my baseball bat, and I'm not afraid to use it. I also have the phone number of a man who said I could ring at any time and he'd leap in his car and come to my rescue.

Only now do I realise that I'd forgotten to call the police. But it can wait until tomorrow. I don't want the real world to intrude in the afterglow of my time with Jamie. And in the calm of my meditation, I am always safe.

45

Knight

The princess gripped her sword in both hands and swung at the monster with all her might. The weapon merely bounced off its scaly hide and jarred her arms. Its slender head spun to face her, and it fixed her with evil red eyes, pinning her in place like a butterfly in a display case. She gulped as it took a deep breath and the furnace inside its belly roared beside her. She glanced towards the forest edge, gauging her chances of escape, but the monster's tail beat lazily like a cat waiting to pounce; even if she escaped the fire, one flick of that tail would send her reeling, possibly never to stand again.

Why did she think she could fight this dragon? No one could prevail against this monster.

The blast came with a great roar, and though she dearly wanted to run in the other direction, the princess ducked beneath the dragon and hid behind a leg as thick as a tree trunk. Though she avoided the flames, the leg raised and lowered, trying to stomp her, and the tail waved faster and stronger. She darted around beneath the dragon, dodging its legs, and wondering when she should take her chance and run to the forest. The beast roared its confusion and anger, and the furnace rumbled again inside it.

The princess ran from beneath the beast and raced towards the forest edge, lifting her skirts as she ran. Her foot caught behind a root and she fell.

Ouff. The ground knocked the air from her lungs.

Ouch. A sharp rock dug into her shoulder.

The dragon bore down on her with murder in its eyes.

The princess scrambled to her feet, but her ankle gave way. She dipped and nearly fell. The dragon's hot breath singed her heels as she staggered towards the trees, certain that her last moments had come.

An almighty roar—a sound fiercer than the dragon's—seared through the landscape. The ground shook. A low white carriage with no horses, a front like bared teeth and a shadowy head set behind a clear screen raced towards her at unbelievable speed. What wizardry was this?

She fell to her knees and buried her face in her arms. The carriage stopped beside her, but she dared not look. Something clicked—a door opening?—and a warm, strong arm wrapped around her and hauled her sideways and up. She gasped and landed on something that closely resembled a man's lap—a lap covered in chain mail. Her knight had come!

Something metallic slammed beside her. She flinched.

'Don't worry, m'lady, you're safe now,' a deep honey-flavoured voice said.

The roar repeated. She lurched forward. A large hand restrained her. She looked up. Flames licked at the windows and Jamie grinned down at her.

'Do you like my nineteen-sixty-nine Charger?' he asked.

My eyes fly open. WHAT! A knight driving a white charger has just rescued me from a fire-breathing dragon! And not just any knight. What was my unconscious mind thinking, turning my handsome locksmith into a knight in shining armour?

No. I will not play the damsel in distress. I'll handle this myself.

As I drift back to sleep, I note that the dream came to me in third person. I'd felt as if I were starring in a story I'd written. I'd even been aware of my own voice narrating it. I congratulated my unconscious mind for recognising the male saviour discourse as merely a cultural vestige, worthy only of a third person narration, not a first person reality. I could sleep safe in the knowledge that I didn't really expect or want someone else to come to my rescue. And I didn't need anyone either.

At least I hoped it wouldn't come to that.

***

Sleep?

If only.

Word-shaped bullets pound against my skull and ricochet again and again. I am not following the thoughts; they just won't stop coming. I'm not thinking about the thoughts; they are fading away, but they keep returning, like some bad guy in a movie that just won't die. The world beneath the veil is so far away that it might as well not exist, and I can't find the entrance. This fact adds immeasurably to my frustration. My mind has gone crazy, and I can't get it under control.

An hour, at least, has passed while I wait for the onslaught to slow. But the thoughts and images just keep spinning and thumping. I'm exhausted, but I can't sleep, and every moment that I lie here waiting to slip into oblivion is precious time wasted. I've been working way too hard—long hours with my concentration too often interrupted by anxiety and irritation at the two men that have turned my life into some kind of hell. And now all the things I need to do and haven't attended to while I focus on the editing are reminding me of their existence. My 'to do' list is overwhelming. It doesn't bother me during the day, but at night, everything becomes urgent. I need to do these things, and somewhere my body feels that it should do them now. But I'm too tired to get up and try to wade through the work.

My confidence is shot. I'm probably making grammar mistakes in the editing, and the retribution when they're found—someone will notice eventually—will be swift and cruel. And I sure as hell aren't managing my mind as I should. I grab my hair at the roots and yank. I tuck my legs underneath me and bury my head in the pillow. Tears threaten. I'm a wreck and I shouldn't be. I should be able to handle this. I know how to handle it, but nothing is working.

I try to take my mind elsewhere with visualisations and mantras. I ignore the thought forms and their accompanying feelings. They do fade, but they come back, as predictable as a yo-yo, and knock the mantras aside. I'm too tired to maintain the concentration required to hold them steady against the barrage.

So I make them the focus of my attention. I wait for the next one. And there is a gap. A blessed space.

I enter the space and find relief, but then, like a set of ocean waves, they rise again in a great swell and crash against the inside of my skull. On the outside, an iron band tightens around my temples. The blood in the veins beneath it pulses like a Japanese drum. My eyes are sore and dry, and even pressing into them with the palm of my hand does not relieve the discomfort.

I have had enough.

ENOUGH!

I will not be at the mercy of my mind. I will not be at the mercy of anyone.

Bring it on; I'm watching. And waiting.

The thoughts go strangely shy.

Where do they come from, anyway?

Where do they stay?

Where do they go?

I slip into the space opened up by the unanswerable questions, and find myself blissfully on the other side.

The clarity is brilliant—but too brilliant. Still I cannot sleep. But it is a better place to spend time while I wait, and I have the satisfaction of knowing that I've taken back control.

However, taking back control of the runaway train of my outer life will not be so easy.

I snort; control is an illusion. Cause and effect and habits drive our lives. I never had a say in the entrance of Dita or Scott into my personal play. I never choreographed them in, but now I must dance around them until they choose to leave, or the scene changes—and it will, eventually. Everything changes.

Thank goodness for that!

46

Man in a Room

My eyes fly open in shock and I stifle a scream. Someone stands at the foot of my bed—a man. I don't dare move, just watch the shadowy figure take form as my eyes adjust to the dark. I can't see his face, but I feel his gaze on me, and though he remains still, he emanates a sense of threat that freezes me to my core.

My eyes fly open and I gasp for breath. I grab my torch from the bedside table, flick it on and shine the beam around the room—nothing. Thank God it was a dream—a dream within a dream. But my heart races as if it'd been real. I sit up, flick off the torch and listen in the darkness for signs of a stalker, but the night is still and silent as death—not even any frogs. No rustle of a wombat passing, and no hoot of an owl or chirp of a ring-tailed possum break the all-encompassing silence. And Merlin sleeps curled up beside me.

Consciously, I might be hiding my fear beneath my bravado and thinking that made me unafraid, but I couldn't fool my dreaming mind. It'd sent me a clear message: pay attention; the fear is real.

I take a deep breath. The stalker is certainly real. But he's not here tonight. My heart rate returns to something closer to normal.

I switch on the torch again and shine it at the clock: 5 AM. A little earlier than usual, but too late to return to sleep, and a prime time for meditation. I climb out of bed, slip on my dressing gown and head for the shrine room.

I love the clarity of the atmosphere at this time of day, before the world awakes. The first light is just touching the ground outside my window, and the birds begin to stir. I rest in a mind as clear and still as the morning. The disturbing events of the night fade into the past—the dreams relegated to another time. All there is now is now. And that's all I need.

One thought emerges from the stillness: I will make my house a fortress and lock myself inside. Yes, that will make me safe. Today, Jamie will replace the ancient locks with their modern counterparts.

Don't think about the thoughts. Just let them go.

Silence.

Stillness.

Clarity.

The sage is dead, but he is also not dead. He lived before his death, and true time knows no order. It does not even exist. Even Slade, though killed off by his author, is still alive somewhere in time.

Silence.

Stillness.

Clarity.

I open my eyes and find myself still sitting in meditation posture before a shrine, but in a dark place. The air is thick, stifling, and cold. The butter lamp burns dangerously low. I must refill it and change the wick before the flame dies completely. To have no flame would be very bad, but the butter is running low and I have no idea how long the storm will last.

I look to the crack above the door in the wooden wall across the front of the cave, seeking indication of the time and state of the snow, but it is so dark and the light so dim that I'm not sure where the door is. After a couple of blinks, I make out the frame on the other side of the small room. No light penetrates the gloom from that direction, or from any direction. The snow has been above the windows for weeks. Only when it closed over the door did I begin to worry. But worry is pointless. The snow will go when it's ready. Nothing I can do will hasten its departure.

It's time to stretch and relieve myself. I carefully refill the lamp and change the wick. I have plenty of those. Then I struggle with the door, heave it open and poke the top of the snow with a stick. It's still ice. Hard as a rock. The only air coming in now is down the narrow crack that forms a kind of a chimney. Nothing goes up anymore. The firewood ran out days ago. My Tsampa will not last much longer either, and I have nothing else. And even if I could chip a bit off, I don't have enough fire to melt the ice for water. I no longer use my precious supply to moisten the Tsampa, and that makes it hard to eat.

A few days ago—or was it a week? Could it be longer? Time has disappeared in this endless night—I was grateful for the safety of the cave as the storm raged outside, but now, this fortress from the elements has become my tomb. I move little, breathe little to use the least possible amount of air and energy, and make the food and water last longer. I pray it will last until I can chip away the ice and crawl from the cave to the stream, but I have only a few mouthfuls of water left and not enough saliva in my mouth to moisten the Tsampa. I haven't eaten for some time, and now my stomach clenches painfully.

When I let my mind roam—only as practice to cut through the stream of thoughts—I smile at my naivety in thinking of this life in a cave as freedom. Freedom from rules and schedules this may be, but it is also freedom to starve. In the monastery, I always had food, always had water, always had sufficient air to breathe. The company I can do without, but the lack of basic necessities makes it hard to keep the mind focused on loftier goals. I am too aware of the cold, the thirst and the hunger.

I never thought it would be this difficult. Fear even sneaks into my mind and curdles the bile in my stomach.

But I am determined to survive, and I will remain focused. My chest barely moves, for there is little air left to breathe, but I will not extinguish the lamp, even though it burns my precious air. I must face my fear. What is death to me, anyway?

I am a chopa, a dharma practitioner. I do not do this for myself. My suffering is nothing compared to the accumulated suffering of all beings, and all my practice—every single moment of mental stillness and clarity, every insight and every chant and stream of light envisaged—is for one purpose only; to benefit beings. In remembering them I forget myself.

I return to my meditation seat.

May all beings enjoy happiness and the causes of happiness.

May they be free from suffering and the causes of suffering.

My heart opens.

The veil parts, and the true nature of existence is laid bare.

Fear does not even exist here.

My body will die, but my mind will continue, as it does now, one moment of consciousness leading to another, like a flame passed from one lamp to another. Even death does not exist here. And life is boundless.

Silence.

Stillness.

Clarity.

The yogi and I are one, yet not the same.

He did not die this way. I know how he died. I sense a glimmer of light at the top of the door, just when he is barely strong enough to struggle to his feet, poke his stick at it and see it fall away. I feel his relief as the fresh air rushes in. He can even see blue sky through the hole.

I hope that my fortress will not become my tomb either.

I feel somehow strengthened by this insight—if that's what it is. Just as he made it through his dark night by remembering his ultimate purpose, I can too. Each time Dita attacks or Scott appears unannounced and unwanted, I'm forced to practice meditation to stave off the corresponding assault on my peace and clarity. My ability to remain in a state of equanimity is what is important, and I'm getting plenty of practice at that.

Silence.
Stillness.
Clarity.
The yogi and I are one, yet not the same.

47

This Way

Merlin pulls against his leash. He's like a pug dog, small and all muscle—he even grunts like one sometimes. He's got a surprising amount of power for a small cat, and he doesn't give up easily. I have to fight to drag him in the direction I want to go.

Part of me screams that I have to get straight to work, but the wiser part points out that I'll work faster and more cleanly if I've had a walk first—and the cat will be less likely to hassle me for attention. The deadline for the editing job is getting closer, but I should make it, unless there's some disaster.

'This way, Merlin,' I say, wanting to see the view over the ocean. I need to experience that vast sense of space again.

But I'm a chopa. I do not do this for myself. My suffering is nothing compared to the accumulated suffering of all beings.

I sigh. Damn the yogi in me.

Fine, what is best for Merlin? Perhaps we can make a compromise. I laugh at that. Who can compromise with a cat? Not me, that's for sure. He's still trying to pull me his way. I loosen the leash and let him lead.

He rushes off to the path along the stream. It leads to the view anyway. I just wanted to get there quicker.

The stream is just a gentle flow now, so different to the raging, post-storm torrent. The green leaves, mottled trunks and dappled brown leaf litter of the forest make it easy to relax. My work is thinning out. I need another job when Kelee's story is done, and I have nothing lined up. I can't help thinking that Dita's attack on my editing skills is hurting my business. I suspect that's his aim with his new campaign. Clearly, he's got a few friends riled up enough to join the bullying. My friends tell me Dita's accomplices are leaving derogatory comments all over the place.

I let the thought drop and focus on not tripping over rocks and roots, but it remains at the bottom of my brain, like mud at the bottom of the pool Merlin's taking a drink from. I'm so sick of Dita's attacks, and now Scott has become a problem as well, it's all a bit much.

Merlin takes off at a run. He drags me up the hill, and though I don't feel like running, I race after him. My only other options are to let the leash go or restrain the cat—a battle I can't see a good reason for.

I stumble on the rough path and twigs grab my hair, but I race on. Merlin's excited now. He stops, fixes me with a manic look, dances sideways with the fur on his spine raised, then sprints off again. I let him pull me along.

It feels like my life.

Out of control.

Who's pulling me? Dita? Scott? God? Karma?

All of them.

Morning sun filters through the trees ahead. It dances on the leaves, kisses the trunks and dapples the ground. The air smells of leaf litter and eucalyptus, but it's fresh and clean.

I let the leash go. I'm sick of battling.

The relief is enormous, and Merlin doesn't run far. The worst scenario doesn't happen. I won't have to scramble through the undergrowth to grab his leash and pull him back to the path.

It takes two to fight.

Perhaps I could loosen up a bit. Perhaps I should.

'Good kitty.' I reach Merlin and give him a stroke. He purrs happily, then lets me lead the rest of the way. I'm in control, he says, I just let you think you are. I decide that it doesn't matter who's in control, we'll get to the same end point whichever route we take.

One way is a battle, the other is the easy route. Is it worth the battle just to go the way I want to go?

48

History

I call the police as soon as I get back from the walk. Merlin has a few cat bickies and settles down on the lambskin for a wash while I tell them I have a stalker and I'm a bit freaked out because I live alone in the bush. They ask me if I have any idea who it is. I tell them and give them his number.

'Okay, we'll look into it and send up a car to have a chat. Will you be home today?'

'Yes, you can come anytime, and thank you for taking it seriously.'

'That's our job, ma'am. Have a good day.'

Ma'am? I wonder if the policeman grew up in Australia. I'd imagined they'd be too busy to take much notice of a woman reporting a stalker, but I'm glad I've done it now.

***

I hear a car, but it's too early for Jamie. He said he'd come after lunch. I peek outside. A white car with a strip of blue checks and the word Police along the

232

side sits at the gate. Both doors open, and out step a man and woman dressed alike in dark blue trousers, big black boots and pale blue shirts with the NSW Police insignia on the sleeves. A few blond strands escape from the woman's dark blue cap, but the headgear—decorated with a stripe of blue and white checks and a silver badge—hides the male cop's hair completely. Handguns safely tucked into black holsters sit on their hips.

My heart does a kind of flip. Seeing them here makes the whole thing far too real. Was that why I kept forgetting to call them? The man opens the gate, and they walk across the grass with the same macho gait. I guess the gun makes it hard to keep your arms close to your body, and the boots look heavy.

I meet them at the door and they introduce themselves, then I show them where I heard the noises outside. They check the security, find it lacking and approve of my upgrade. When we return to the front door after a full circuit of the rambling house, the man, whose name I've already forgotten, says he'd like to ask a few more questions, so I sit them down at the table and chairs on the veranda and tell them about our date and Scott's first visit here. The woman takes notes on a small yellow pad of paper.

'Did you see actually him the second time?' she asks.

I shake my head. 'But I knew it was him. Who else could it be?'

'A positive identification would be helpful,' the man said. 'Then we could pay him a visit.'

'That might make it worse.'

The woman glances at the man and he nods so slightly that I almost miss it. Some pre-arranged signal. I frown, wondering what's next.

'We checked him out,' the woman says. 'Unfortunately, he has a record.'

I sit straighter in the chair and steel myself for the worst.

'He's had restraining orders taken out on him by his ex-wife and another woman as well. The last one was a year ago.'

'A serial stalker. Great.'

The woman nods; her eyes show she feels for me. I could ask, but I'm not sure I want to know the details. She tells me anyway. 'Domestic violence, then stalking. He's a mean bastard beneath that pretty veneer.'

I assume his picture is on his file.

'We suggest that you take one out as well,' the policeman says.

'Do they work?'

'They allow us to make it clear to the perpetrators of violent or intimidating behaviour that it is a criminal offence and they will be prosecuted should it continue.'

'In other words, no.'

The woman: 'They can be very effective in some situations.'

'What about in his situations? Did he breach them?'

The woman nods. 'That's why they're on his record.'

The man: 'If he does return, try to get a look at him. That's all we need to act.'

'But don't endanger yourself.' The woman again.

'What happens if he gets caught?'

'He paid a six thousand dollar fine both times. If he does it again, it'll be anywhere from two months to two years in jail.'

'He only escaped a jail term the second time, because …' the woman checks a page at the back of her notebook, 'he has ultradian cycling bipolar disorder and he agreed to stay on his medication.'

'Ultradian cycling?'

'Means he can change from manic to depressive and back again pretty fast. I interviewed a man with bi-polar once, he said it was hard to stay on his medication because it took the fun out of life.' She shrugged in a what-can-you-say-to-that kind of way.

Poor Scott. I recalled my interactions with him. He'd been subdued but not depressed, normal really, on the date—on his medication perhaps—but after that, he'd swung from guilty, pessimistic and sad to super-confident, energetic and aggressive. How long might a manic episode last? How dangerous might he get? I needed to do some research.

'We have the paperwork with us if you want to start the ball rolling.' The man said. I'm getting whiplash turning from one neat blue uniform to another. They look tough. And, clearly, Scott is a lot more dangerous than I'd thought. I could do with some muscle on my side.

'Yeah. I'll do that. How long does it take?'

'Given his history, we can do an Interim Police Restraining Order that will take effect immediately and last seventy two hours.'

'Do I have to go to court?'

'Only if you want it to continue, and it's only before the local judge, but we hope that our involvement, even on an interim order, may be enough to keep him away. It will certainly alert him to the serious nature of his behaviour.'

The woman pulls a brochure from her satchel and hands it to me. 'All the information is there.'

'Hopefully, this will scare him off and you'll have no more problems,' the male cop says. 'We'll also encourage him to take his medication when we deliver it, but if he shows, ring us straight away.'

The cop car drives back up the driveway, and I head to my computer to get some work done before the gorgeous locksmith arrives.

But before I begin, I do a little research on ultradian cycling bipolar disorder. Some of the words used to describe manic episodes are a little scary: impulsiveness, poor judgement, reckless behaviour and, in severe cases, delusions and hallucinations. I hope Scott doesn't have a severe case, and that he decides to take his tablets. Should I ring him and encourage him? Would that help? I can see how difficult it must be to live with something like that, but I don't trust my ability to handle it at all.

I should at least do some meditation for him, but I really can't afford the time now. The cops took up time I'd planned to use editing.

I realise what I just thought and shake my head. Where is my concern for others? The yogi in me is disappointed at my selfishness. It need not take long, he reminds me. I don't even have to move from my seat.

I visualise Scott filled with the symptoms of his disorder in the form of black swirling smoke.

Inhale: the black smoke curls into my heart centre and dissolves into the space of love that resides there.

Exhale: a stream of healing white light flows from my heart into Scott and floods him with a love so profound that it washes away his darkness and fills him with light.

I repeat the visualisation a few times, riding it on my breath, then, having found some measure of peace, I get back to work.

49

Deal

I have a review from a couple of weeks ago that I've forgotten to post, and I want to get that out of the way, so I click on my Amazon bookmark first. It takes me to the *Catnip Creek* page. Before I press Enter to search for the relevant book, I happen to notice that the number of reviews has risen. I scroll down and discover another one star review.

My heart sinks, but I take a deep breath and remind myself that you can't please everyone. My book's good, I know that. A publisher wouldn't have picked it up if it wasn't. A low-starred review could just be from someone who doesn't like it. Maybe they prefer thrillers.

I take a deep breath and raise my eyes to the photo of my lama before reading. His image reminds me of everything he's ever taught me. This is just another opportunity to practice—manure to make this rose bloom.

If you are looking for an alternative to conventional an-esthetics or sleep medication and are looking for the shortest possible path to unconsciousness, look no further than Catnip Creek by Prunella Smith. A book has never so failed to 'start' in the entirety of recorded literary history. From page one it will be clear to the reader that Ms Smith is either a child author or possibly suffering from some mental trauma. You will ask yourself how a work so trivial and bland could have been created using the English language. You will laugh. You will cry. Never for the right reasons. It is likely that you will call your friends, only to tell them that you have indeed found a book so boring and tasteless that it may have medical applications. Going in for dental work? No problem. Read a chapter of this book and NEVER FEEL ANYTHING EVER AGAIN.

The story is of two elderly people: Carl and Clarissa (the author clearly has an alliteration fetish) who have a cat named Hubert. Are you asleep already? So was I. Sloshing through this book was so uncomfortable and nauseating that at times I thought suicide would be my only escape from a world in which this person is considered an author. Further, it infuriates me that she believes not only that she is a writer, but that she has the gall to judge the work of other, more-talented authors in her reviews.

Trust me when I say if the option for zero stars was available, I would select it. I encourage people to stay away from this book and this author, unless your goal is to have every single one of your sensibilities offended. As a reader, as a fan of literature and as a person, I feel like I have lost half a day of my life that I will never get back. I am ashamed to admit that I read this book.

I shake my head in a mixture of disbelief and sadness, not for me, but because it's a pity Dita's book isn't as entertaining as the review. Maybe he didn't write it. I don't know. Whoever did, it's obvious they haven't read the book. He'd mention the killer dung beetle for sure if he had. I have to believe it's Dita using another account—the review is by Razor Sharp—or someone he's put up to it.

I click on the report as inappropriate button, but know I'll have to do more. I'll compose a letter that tells the review moderation team all about the abuse just as soon as I've finished the editing job. It will take too much time to do it now. With Scott's presence so much more tangible, I'm not even sure I care anymore.

At least my ability to dip beneath the veil is improving; and there's Jamie—a ray of sunshine in a dark time.

The landline rings. I pick it up.

'Hi El, it's Liz.'

'Hi.' We'd exchanged texts earlier, and I'd told her I phoned the cops.

'Is everything okay?'

'Yeah. No. Well ...'

'What? Spill it.'

'No stalker, so I'm fine on that front but ... I just got another one star review.'

'Oh. I'm sorry to hear that.'

'Perhaps I should stop trying to provide real critical appraisal in public.'

Silence.

'Liz?'

'Did you get control of your website back?'

'Yeah, that's all fine, I have a good techy friend.' I'm wondering where she's going with this.

'Listen … don't take this the wrong way, but … usually, I'd tell you to stick to your guns, but maybe you just don't need this kind of shit right now.'

'You can say that again.'

'If Dita put him up to it, you could get more like this … Maybe just take the guy's review down. I mean, is it worth it? Really? The fighting with these people?'

'I … I used to think so, but I'm not so sure right at the moment.'

'Give yourself a break. You don't have to single-handedly right the inequities of the system.'

'No, I don't.' I suddenly feel really tired. What a shitty day. Looks like karma is biting me in the butt. But my intention in writing honest reviews is good, so the outcome in the end should be good. I hope. 'But I'd be letting a bully get his way,' I say. 'I can't do that. It'd be telling him his tactics work and he'll just do it again.'

'Maybe that's not your problem.'

'But it's making it more likely it'll be someone else's problem.'

'Just swallow your pride and it'll all be over.'

Pride? Was this about pride? No. It didn't feel like that. 'It's not pride; it's principles, and fighting injustice.'

'Sure, but in the end, you have to swallow your pride to admit that in this instance sticking to your principles might not be the best course of action. And you'd be practising non-violence, you know, stopping a fight before someone—you—gets hurt. You even admitted it's a fight, and no one wins a fight. You taught me that.'

Now it's my turn to be quiet.

'Ella? … Just think about it, okay? I have to go, but if you don't feel safe, you're welcome to stay with me.'

'Okay.' We say our goodbyes and hang up, and I realise that I didn't tell her what the cops said about Scott. It's best she doesn't know, anyway. She'll only worry.

By tonight though, I'll have good strong locks on the door.

Merlin jumps onto the desk and gives me a smooch. I scratch him under the ears and wonder what to do about the stalkers—both of them; all of them. My life is unravelling.

I certainly would feel better if I got rid of one of them. And what is the point of this life, anyway? It has nothing to do with winning battles over reviews. I stare into the garden and return to my mental home. The place where everything is well. One of my stalkers might not be that difficult to deal with. Deal. That's the word.

***

I click through to my Amazon account, find where my reviews are stored and delete the cause of Dita's torment. It's strangely easy to do, and I don't feel as though I've lost a battle; I feel as if a load has been lifted off my chest.

Why didn't I do it earlier?

I still believe all those things about the necessity of real critical appraisal in the business, but ... why should I put myself in the line of fire? Am I a coward now? Does it matter?

50

Kelee's World

Kelee knelt before the grave and stared at Slade's name carved on the piece of granite. Wind gusted through the trees and tossed her tresses across her face. Strands stuck in her tears and she brushed them away. She still didn't believe it. Slade's death seemed unreal, as if it had happened to someone else, as if he was still alive somewhere that she couldn't reach.

She shook her head and wiped her sleeve across her eyes. What was the point of tears? They didn't solve anything. She was done with them. All cried out anyway.

Her life had stopped, almost as if she'd died with him. Part of her had, for sure. Her future was now a blank slate, all possibility of a life with Slade shattered. But she could not return to her old life. In the face of Slade's death, her old concerns seemed trivial.

A spit of rain fell. Storm clouds rolled across the sky and the day darkened prematurely. Kelee drew her velvet cloak closer around her. What use was the Menhir clasp at her throat? Being the chief's daughter hadn't made her any happier—quite the opposite—and it wouldn't make a bit of difference when she died; she'd still end up in the ground like everyone else. Nothing remained here for her now.

The parents she'd loved had not lifted a finger to save her love when he'd been wrongly accused, and their apparent capitulation to her statement that she would never marry Beak was likely a ruse to placate her until she 'got over' her loss. She would never get over her loss.

What would she do from now until she joined Slade in death?

When she lay dying, what would she see when she looked back over her life? Would it have been a life worth living? Or would it have been a waste? Would she die in peace like Slade, despite his pain? Or would she scream and rail against existence like the man she'd left pinned beneath the horse?

Slade had been a secret Warrior. Miramar was a Warrior. Kelee admired them both for their kindness, their fortitude in the face of trials and their wisdom. Could Kelee Menhir dedicate herself to helping others as Miramar did? That would be a fine monument to Slade's death.

She would go to Sheldra; not to escape her father, not even to spite him—though he would see it as a betrayal—but to become a Warrior.

'Nonsense. I would never have been so passive. I would have been angry.'
Kelee.

I smile. Though my eyes are fixed on the words on my computer screen, I see Kelee in my mind, and her reality feels as firm as my own. 'That isn't you,' I say. 'It's a fictional you. And a fictional story.'

I would have clawed Beak's eyes out. Why does that woman think that to have a partner makes you weaker? It is not so.'

I shrug. 'Her beliefs are her own.' I smile at my use of Magan speech patterns.

'If Slade dies, so do all the people he saves at the Battle of Craggin Plain.'

Book three, *Demon's Grip*. I wonder if Tanya got that tale right. 'This story will not change yours,' I tell her. 'I'm sure of it. This is no longer your and Slade's story.'

Kelee nods. *'That Kelee is most definitely not me.'*

'At most, the author created an alternate reality when she allowed Slade to die, but the events in that reality won't affect your reality. Your life has already happened, and in your reality he lived.'

'Thank the Pathmaker.'

I scan back over the passage. It seems a little contrived, and I don't doubt that Kelee's real story would be better. She's a strong woman whether she has a man with her or not.

'My path to awareness was slower, but it was my path and I was sure of every step.'

She seems to have read my mind. Not surprising given the internal mode of our communication. 'I suspect that the end result will be the same in both stories.'

She shakes her long black hair. *'The destination may be the same, but one's experience of it differs depending on the route one takes to get there.'*

True.

'I don't like that this author has created an alternate version of events. She has diminished my story.'

'Artists create new worlds with every work, but they don't affect our world.'

'Don't they?' Her steely green eyes fix on me, as if to say, think about it.

She has a point. Wouldn't the nineteen-nineties generation be different without Harry Potter's story? But I'm trying to mollify her. 'I doubt it would go so far as to cause someone's death.'

She shrugs. 'Their imaginations would be different, and everything is created from imagination. Belief is a powerful thing.'

'But the past can't be changed.'

'Can't it? Do you know for sure?'

'In your world, Slade lived. If that changes, it's a different world, an alternate reality.' I wonder if he's still alive.

'His life hangs in the balance.'

She definitely read my mind.

'He has an illness, and I fear that his death in an alternate reality will weaken him further.'

Now I understand her urgency, but does the written word have that much power? Kelee says nothing, but images of books that have moved millions flood my mind. I think of how newspapers and magazines can twist the truth and manipulate public opinion, and how the web hosts millions of self-styled experts whose blogs stir readers' passions. Yes, the written word has great power, and too many take anything written as gospel.

'If you don't present an alternative, people will believe whatever is placed before them.' She fixes her big green eyes on me with a silent plea.

'I'm not the author.'

'No, I am.'

And I've done what I can already.

'Speak to her, let her hear the truth. Spoken aloud, it will lessen her attachment to her version, and once heard, the power of its truth will counteract her version to some degree.'

Wow. I've never thought about such things before. I can't help wondering what would happen if the story becomes famous and thousands of people believe that Slade dies.

'It won't; people won't like it enough. They want to see the lovers together. But it would be best for Slade's health if it isn't published in its present form.'

I imagine myself phoning Tanya—that is what Kelee wants—and explaining all this in another attempt to get her to write the story Kelee's way—hell, it is her story. But it's weird enough when an author talks to their own characters; I'm talking to another author's character and believing in her existence apart from the story! Nah. It would never work. I'd just lose a client.

'*Thanks,*' Kelee says. And she's gone. Vanished from my mind. The refrain from a Disney song from Peter Pan dances in.

… If you believe in fairies, just clap your hands; clap, clap, clap.

I shake my head and roll my eyes. Part of me wonders if I'm cracking up, but I know I'm not. I just have an active imagination and a strong belief that Kelee's story—whether it has any reality apart from fiction or not—will be stronger if Slade lives.

Clap. Clap. Clap.

I guess I could try one more time.

51

Shots

'I must have read it a million times before I sent it,' I tell Jamie as he reads the email I sent to Dita on my tablet. 'And then I kept wondering if I'd done the right thing. I caved, turned my back on my principles.'

He shakes his head and hands me back the tablet. 'I think you're just simplifying your life.'

'Yeah, I figured if I could get one bully off my back, I'd be making progress. And the editing slander was likely to lose me clients. I can't afford that.'

We sit on the couch, staring at the fire. Our bellies are full with a dinner he helped cook, the new locks are installed and the story fully told. I completed a good chunk of the editing job while he worked on the locks so I'm enjoying a well-earned evening off. We've covered a lot of ground since I agreed to let him stay— I decided I didn't need to prove my independence to anyone, least of all myself, and that it was sensible to take the policeman's professional advice. Their visit had brought home to me that Scott wasn't just some slightly off man; I was dealing with someone guilty of criminal charges. I actually did need help, and it didn't diminish me to accept it when offered.

'Did you ever have a white Charger?' I ask.

His eyebrows fly up and a grin sweeps across his face like a warm wind on a cold day. 'I did, actually, a nineteen-sixty-nine model, back when I was into big angry cars.'

I nearly choke on the hot chocolate I'm taking a sip of.

'Why did you ask?'

'Um, just a stray question.'

He narrows his eyes at me. I'll have to do better than that.

'Fine. I had a dream. I was a princess fighting a dragon, and you drove up in a—'

Merlin leaps up from his place at the fire and races to the window. He sits on the platform on top of his scratching post and growls.

'White Charger?' Jamie finishes while we both stare at the cat.

I nod. My heart's racing, but I remind myself that the doors are all deadlocked and I'm not alone.

'I don't know what's stranger,' Jamie continues, 'that you dreamt about a car I used to own or that your cat acts like a dog.'

'Or that there's probably someone out there.'

'That too. Shouldn't they have delivered the restraining order by now?'

'Their boss had already signed it to make it quick. They were going to deliver it as soon as they left here.'

'Two-timing bitch!' someone yells from outside. 'I should have known it was you!'

We spring to our feet. 'The guy is totally deluded,' I say.

'They're the most dangerous ones,' Jamie says.

'Not helping.'

'Is it him?'

'Sounds like it.'

'Is aural recognition enough for the cops?'

I smile at his awesome vocabulary.

'What?'

'Nothing. They asked me to try to get a visual.'

Now he smiles.

'What?'

'You sound like a cop show.'

I draw a blank.

'Get a visual. That's cop speak.'

'I guess it is.' He even hears word usage. I'm falling in love.

'You really think taking it down now will make it all better!' Scott's angry voice slices the still night like a knife through flesh. 'You ruined my career, you vindictive bitch.'

I flinch. *Ruined his career?* 'Dita?' *He couldn't be. Could he?* I turn to Jamie. He shrugs.

I shake my head, disbelieving, and at the same time realising that I'd only assumed the disgruntled author was American. I hadn't read Dita's bio, hadn't wanted to know anything about him.

'I said you'd be sorry,' Scott shouts from far too close.

Scott or Dita, at this moment, it doesn't matter who he is; I want to shout at him, tell him to piss off, but the cops said not to engage him, and I know that's best, so I take a deep breath, clear my mind and head towards the land-line—the reception isn't good enough on my smart phone. But when I walk past the uncurtained window between the lounge and the office, a crack splits the night and shatters the window. I scream and duck, my mind whirling. That gun is real. This is not a scene in a book, not a dream, not a memory or a vision. This is real. My life. Now. Damn.

'Shit! He has a gun,' Jamie says. 'Stay down.'

Duh! I'm flat on the floor and couldn't move if I wanted to—which I don't.

'Do you have a gun?' he asks.

'Why the hell would I have a Goddamned gun?'

'Farmers have them to shoot rabbits.'

'I am so *not* a farmer. What would you do with it anyway? Shoot him?'

'Self-defence.' He shrugs again.

'No one writes bad things about me and gets away with it,' Scott shouts.

The realisation lands in my stomach like a lump of lead. Two of my worlds collide and a shiver races up my spine. 'He's Dita; he has to be. It doesn't make sense otherwise,' I say, reeling with a mixture of shock, amazement and the fading vestiges of disbelief.

'Pen name?' Jamie suggests.

I nod. We never did share surnames. Though Davidson, Dita's surname, could be as fake as Dita. I snort at the realisation that he can hardly say I ruined his career, when he could start again with a new name. But anger is ignorant, it wouldn't see that. The venom of Dita's online abuse funnels into my perception of the man I know as Scott, and surprisingly, the completed picture makes sense—Dita's vitriol is a perfect expression of Scott's mixture of insecurity and anger. *I'm the vindictive old biddy he was looking for!* The realisation prickles my skin.

I have no photos of me on the internet—Merlin's my gravatar—so Dita had no idea what I might look like. But the physical safety of the internet world is gone now, my anonymity and the barrier between the worlds shattered like the window. The beast is loose. My nightmare has become real. *How did he find out?*

Another crack, and the window by the TV explodes. Now Jamie's on the floor. 'Shit. Fuck. He got me, the bastard!'

'Christ, Jamie! Is it bad?'

'Nah, just grazed my shoulder. Don't worry about me. Call the cops.'

I'm relieved and worried at the same time: Jamie saved me from the quandary of trying to decide which way to go, but those shots came close together; they had to be from a semi-automatic, most likely a pistol since semi-automatic rifles were outlawed after the Port Arthur Massacre. The only people allowed pistols are target shooters, and that means that the man is quite possibly lethal.

I crawl towards the phone. My heart is knocking so hard against my ribs, I'm scared they'll break. I make it to the phone, but the line is dead. Jesus. My life is turning into a thriller! My smart phone only works in the other end of the house, but there're no curtains in the studio I have to walk through, and I haven't drawn them in the far room. I'll be a sitting … er, running, or crawling duck.

Crack. The gun is getting closer. Jamie groans. I peek around the door. Expletives are flying thick and fast in the living room. Jamie's gripping his shoulder and there's blood on his leg as well. I gasp at the sight; that blood is real, not make-up in a movie.

'The bastard's trying to kill me!'

My thought exactly. 'Hang in there. I'm getting help.' I bite my lip, grab my phone and race from the study and down the corridor. It will take the cops at least fifteen minutes to get here, and even the fancy new locks can't keep Scott out now. I hide behind the bed in the spare room and pray that it's a good day for reception. Either way, it's still a bad day for me.

The cops made me program their direct line number into my phone before they left. I'm guessing they didn't trust the restraining order. I bring it up and press call.

No networks found.

'Ella,' Jamie calls. 'He's in the house.'

I try again. No networks found.

Crack. The shot came from inside the house, and I can't be caught down here with no exit. The window has a three metre drop because the ground slopes away. I don't fancy my chances of running away after taking that way out.

I press the green button again. This time the call goes through. A shout of abuse from Scott punctuates my plea for help. The receptionist says they'll be there right away. 'We need an ambulance too. My friend's been shot.'

'I'll arrange that,' she says. 'Stay out of sight.'

I run, bent over, from the room, hoping he can't see me above the window sills, then I realise he's inside now. My heart's thumping at one hundred miles an hour. I run in the direction of Jamie's voice. The shooting has stopped. Does that mean he's dead?

How did Scott get a gun anyway? With his kind of history, it can't be legal.

Suddenly, I feel really ill. This is no novel. This is my reality. The truth of my mortality hits me like a punch in the gut. I have to find Jamie and get out of here.

I know the tracks through the bush, could find my way even in the dark. And the moon is full. We can hide until the cops come. But first, we have to get out.

I sidle along the hall and grab a coat from the hook as I pass the back door. I slip it on while I creep along. The house is silent now apart from the occasional creak near where I heard the last shot. The bathroom door is open, so I slip inside, ease the cupboard open and grope around until I feel the bandages. I grab a couple of big rolls and stuff them into pockets. Anything more will have to wait. He could be dead already for all I know.

Someone's moving in the study. I peek around the door. A figure with a handgun stands silhouetted against the moonlit sky through the window. He bends down and pokes beneath the desk with the barrel. Jamie wouldn't have gone in there, it's a dead end. I creep back the way I've come and spot him peeking out of the bedroom. I run to him, grab his arm and pull him down the corridor to the back door. He limps along, and Scott shouts from behind us.

Another shot rings out and splinters the door jamb behind us as we duck outside. I wrap Jamie's arm over my shoulder and help him stay upright and moving while we run to the cover of the garden shed.

A dark, human-shaped blob wearing a hoody races after us. A bullet hits the earth by my heels and splatters mud up my leg. That was far too close! I jump, dancing over more bullets, and push Jamie forward.

We make it to the shed and rest for a moment with our backs against the tin. Our breaths are coming sharp and fast.

'We have to get into the forest and hide,' I say.

He nods. The muscles on his face are tight.

'Ready?' I ask.

He nods again and picks something off the ground.

I peek around the corner of the shed. A bullet whizzes past my head. Shit!

Jamie holds up a lump of wood and hurls it onto the roof of the garage.

The next shot hits the garage. We grin at each other.

'Go,' I say.

Jamie dashes for the forest. Even injured, the boy can run; thank God. I follow him, but Scott's shouts follow me. He's seen us.

My feet pound the earth, jarring my bones. The monster closes in behind me, his footsteps getting louder. At least he isn't shooting while he runs.

I make it to the forest but trip and stumble over a fallen branch, only just saving myself from a fall. No knight in shining armour drives up in a white charger this time. This is real—far too real. I can't get my head around it.

I look desperately for somewhere to hide, somewhere to escape the beast coming our way.

Jamie stumbles and falls. I haul him up.

'Can't go too far,' he gasps.

I remember the rock. It isn't far, if I can find it in the dark. 'Don't need to,' I whisper. 'This way.'

I wrap his arm over my shoulder again—thank goodness he's not a huge bloke—and help him towards the largest rock in the forest.

52

Confrontation

A large tree nestles close behind the rock, surrounded by a lantana bush. I push into the lantana, dragging Jamie with me. The sticky plant scratches my face and hands and grabs at my hair. We squeeze between the trunk and the rock, then sit side by side with our backs against the rock, trying to still our gasping breaths.

I realise that he's shivering in shock. I take off my jacket and wrap it around him. He tries to protest, but I silence him with a finger on his lips and tell him to lie in recovery position. He doesn't complain.

I don't have a white charger, but I have two rolls of bandages that I wrap around his leg until they're all used up. I'm pretty sure I manage to stop the bleeding. Occasionally, he lets out a muffled groan, as if through lips pressed tightly together. He must be hurting like hell.

The beast crashes through the undergrowth and draws closer, shouting abuse. Fear races through me. The guy has totally lost it. If he finds us here, we could die. No, I don't doubt it; we will die.

I don't want to die, but Scott is coming this way. I have to do something, but my mind has gone numb and I'm shaking all over. What would Kelee do? I wonder. But I have no magic wand. What about the yogi?

I ignore the crashing in the undergrowth, take a deep breath, close my eyes and return myself to the space of stillness that I know so well.

He wouldn't think of himself.

I glance down at Jamie. My fear is nothing compared to the pain he must be feeling. He's not moving anymore, and I suspect he's passed out. He's completely helpless like this.

In remembering him, I forget myself and my fear turns to clarity. A survival instinct I didn't know I had kicks in from deep within, and I give myself over to it.

I crawl back through the lantana, pick up a sharp-edged rock and stand in the deep shadow at the edge of the shrubbery. I grasp the boulder firmly and press back against the rock as the footsteps slow and creep closer. I wait in readiness, unmoving. Since when did my breathing sound so loud?

I do not do this for myself. The thought gives me courage.

Snap. My heart jumps. That was too close.

I peek through a scraggle of lantana and hold my breath. The beast stands at the corner of the big rock. He cocks his head and sniffs. A terrible sense of déjà vu comes over me. I shiver.

I press my lips together and breathe in slowly—
and far too lightly, but I cannot risk him hearing me.
He steps closer. I stay where I am, but raise my arm,
the rock clenched in tight fingers. I'm counting on the
element of surprise, and hoping I'll hit him hard
enough to knock him out.

If he doesn't shoot me first.

A twig snaps. Another step closer.

I hold my breath. My eyes grow wider. My
muscles coil ready to spring. How close should I let him
get? How long should I wait? Should I attempt this at
all? He's big and I'm small. I might just manage to make
him really angry. Time stops, races, and slows all at
once. A tight steel band encases my chest.

I must face my fear. *But what is death to me, anyway? I am a chopa.*

This is not real.

This is real.

This is not 'both real and not real'.

And it is not 'neither real nor not real'.

The understanding clears my mind completely.
Fear no longer exists.

The forest becomes luminous and my awareness as crisp as a frosty morning. My breathing eases,
becomes slow and steady.

I am not afraid to die. It's only the zero to life's
one. Only the off to the circuit's on. One does not exist
without the other.

Still. I wait.

I don't think I can hit him anymore, but I trust I won't have to.

There is no one here, after all. I smile and project the thought like an arrow into his brain.

There really is no one here.

This is not a lie. I am, after all, no one, and I am completely beyond concepts of here and not here. The power of this confidence is extraordinary. It's as if I've made myself completely invisible.

Rustle. The monster stops.

Thump, thump, thump. A wallaby flees through the forest, its signature sound unmistakable.

Rustle, rustle, tromp, tromp, tromp.

Scott takes a step towards the wally.

I lower the rock and breathe freely again. Thank God.

Jamie groans.

Scott stops and turns. 'I know you're there,' he says, aiming the gun at the space beside me. He can't see me in the shadow, but I can see him. The moonlight filters through the trees and hits the side of his face. His eyes are bulging with anger. He moves the gun across the shadows. I dare not breathe. 'Why do you hate me?' His voice is a painful mixture of anger and vulnerability.

I press my lips together, focus on retaining the feeling of invisibility, and visualise him walking away.

'If you don't answer, I'll blast this whole rock with bullets. I have another clip, and I won't stop shooting until you and your … boyfriend'—he spat the word—'are dead. You'll be nothing but a spatter of blood and gore.'

I swallow in a throat gone dry. 'I don't hate you,' I whisper. What choice do I have?

He aims the gun directly at me. 'You hated my book and you wouldn't let me see you.'

My eyes lock on the barrel and I can't stop shivering. I am so not invisible. 'You acted strange. I was scared, that's all; and I didn't hate your book; I just pointed out its faults.'

'In bloody public!' His shout brings another groan from Jamie. The gun swings towards the sound.

'I'm sorry,' I say quickly, drawing the gun back to me.

'Not good enough,' he retorts. 'You ruined my career!'

What career? I think, unable to stop the snark in me having her say. Fair enough under the circumstances.

'Embarrassed me in front of my friends,' he continues. 'I should kill you for that!'

'Don't you think that might be a little bit excessive,' I say. 'You've caused me plenty of damage already.'

'I don't care what you think; you don't know shit.'

'I truly am sorry. I never meant to hurt you.' The gun lowers slowly; I have to keep him talking.

'You're only saying that so I won't kill you.' The gun whips back up again. *Damn.*

'No. I really meant to help you.'

'By leaving a two star review!' His voice rises again and the gun jabs towards me. 'Did you really think that wouldn't hurt?'

'Professional authors take it as part of the job.' I grimace. *Probably shouldn't have said that.*

'So now you're calling me an amateur,' he says through clenched teeth.

Yes, because clearly that's what you are. 'No, I'm just suggesting that you take it as someone's personal opinion and move on. Free speech and all that. People will forget about it soon enough, anyway.'

'Not if it's still there—a stain on my record, a warning flag for buyers. This book stinks. You couldn't have said it clearer.'

'I never used those words.'

'It's still the meaning. Anyone can see that.'

That's because it's the truth. 'I've taken it down, anyway.'

'Too late. The damage has been done.' He jerks the gun in emphasis.

I flinch. Sure, for a moment, that my time has come.

'I should kill you for it.'

He doesn't though. 'You're going to shoot me for writing an honest review?'

Silence.

'Look, you're a good bloke at heart.' I blurt out, instinctively appealing to his better nature. 'Why don't you let me help you with the book?' I can't believe I said that, but my mouth seems to be moving of its own accord. 'We can have a business relationship.' *No, no; I do not want any kind of relationship with this man!* I'm amazed at what I've just said and already regret it, but I do manage to add a clarification. 'You pay me; I help you write better.'

He snorts. 'Trying to barter for your life now, huh?'

I shrug. There is that. But, actually, I think the Buddhist in me took over. 'No.' I lie. 'I think you have a unique perspective on the world. You feel deeply and that gives you material to write from. If you could draw on that emotional depth, you could write something really powerful.' That was true. Whether he'd ever gain the skills to do so was debatable, but it would be good therapy for him anyway.

The gun lowers slightly.

Crazy as it was, the offer may have just saved my life.

'You'd have to take your medication regularly, though,' I add, backtracking just a little.

'What do you know about my medication?' He growls out the words, but the gun stays down.

'Just that life will be easier for you if you take it.'

'It dulls my senses, saps my creativity.'

'We can work with that. My offer stands if you take your medication; otherwise, I can't help you. It's up to you, but we can turn this around, make something good out of it.'

He crumbles to the ground, bows his head and sobs. 'I thought you'd be an ugly old school marm with thick stockings, clumpy shoes and grey hair,' he mumbles between sniffs.

My jaw drops, and I stand there like an idiot, just staring at the unloved little boy who has replaced the monster. Then my compassion kicks in and I kneel before him.

Should I touch him? I'm too scared. I have no idea how to handle this, no idea what he might do. I want to try to take the gun from his hand—it's resting on his lap. I reach out, slowly.

Sirens wail in the valley.

Scott/Dita's head jerks up. His eyes glow wild in the moonlight. He jumps to his feet and glances behind him, then back to me. 'You bitch! You called the cops!'

He lashes out with the gun, hits me across the temple and runs into the bush. 'Ow! Shit! Dammit!' I stagger back against the rock, pain throbbing through my skull, and literally 'seeing stars'. I touch the tender spot, feeling the bump rising already, and my fingers come away wet and sticky. I slide down the rock and join Jamie on the ground, fighting to stay conscious.

At least I'm not dead. I focus on my lama's face, grateful that I, not him, am the one that's bruised and bloodied. My worlds seem to be colliding. My memory of the sage helps me retain my composure while I force my eyes to stay open. If they close, I may never wake up.

I could do with Miramar's healing skills right about now.

Scott's crashing steps fade into the distance. The sirens draw closer, their sound piercing the still night air with a surreal clarity. A car rumbles into life and drives up the road.

We stay there, side by side, listening. At least I listen. I'm pretty sure Jamie's unconscious, which is probably best. He won't feel anything that way. I reassure myself that his breathing is strong, and the medics will be here soon.

I'm not capable of doing anything else anyway. My head's pounding, like someone's taken a jackhammer to my skull. Yeah, right—Dita, of course. I hope he's satisfied now he's had his revenge.

Scott's long gone by the time the ambulance and cop cars pull into the parking area and cut their sirens. Jamie moves slightly and winces.

'We're safe,' I tell him. The moon has moved enough for me to see him manage a small smile.

I leave Jamie, his lips clamped against the pain, and stagger out to greet the cops. They pull their guns. I raise my hands.

'Identify yourself.'

'Um, Prunella Smith. My friend's been shot, he's over there.' I point into the bush.

The cops holster their weapons and the paramedics move into action.

53

Morning

We both spent the night in hospital. Me for observation—I had mild concussion—and Jamie for obvious reasons. The doctors didn't let me see him because I'm not a relative, and they thought I should stay in bed. They also said he needed to sleep, and I figured he'd be doped up on painkillers anyway. One bullet tore right through his shoulder—luckily it missed the bone—and another ripped a hole in his calf, but the emergency ward doctor assured me he'd heal just fine.

I'd phoned Liz, who wasn't too pleased to be woken up at two a.m. but was terribly worried and very pleased to help when she heard the story. She called first thing to tell me that she'd driven up to my place, managed to coax Merlin out from under the bed and had taken him home with her. She also owned up to being the reason Dita Davidson found Prunella Smith. She'd bumped into him in the supermarket and he'd asked if she knew Prunella Smith; she'd said, 'Ella? Sure. You know her too. You went out with her.'

Now I'm at the hospital, free to go—with a warning to call a doctor if I have any dizzy spells or if the headache gets worse—waiting for someone to take me to Jamie. I'm perched on the edge of a plastic chair alone in a sterile waiting room.

A woman walks in with a baby in her arms. He—or is it a she?—looks at me and smiles a gummy smile. I smile back, and for the first time in my life, I think a baby is actually kind of cute. Maybe they're not just screaming poo bags. Maybe I can see myself with one in my arms—one of my own. I could try just one. If I found the right man.

'You here for James Claypole?' a male voice asks from the doorway.

I look over. He's holding one side of the double doors open. 'Yeah.'

The nurse jerks his head towards the corridor. 'You can see him now. He's still a bit sleepy, but he'll be okay in a few hours. We'll keep him in one more night though, just in case. This is the first bullet wound any of us have seen.' The guy prattles on while I follow him down the corridor with my eyes straight ahead. I do not want to see the sick and injured people in the rooms we pass.

He leads me into a four-bed ward with curtains drawn around the beds, shielding the occupants from sight, and holds back the first curtain. I step inside the enclosure and look at the bed with a lump in my throat. 'Half an hour only, please,' the nurse says. 'He's had a major trauma and needs to rest.' He waits for my nod, then leaves us to it.

Jamie is lying on his back with his eyes closed. I'm not even sure he's awake, though he looks peaceful enough. I walk close and lean over, barely breathing. A grin spreads across his face.

'Sorry I couldn't ride up in my white charger and save the day,' he says.

I jump back. 'Jeez, you gave me a fright!'

'Why? Did you think I was dead?'

'Course not; I thought you might be asleep.'

'It'd take more than a mad man with a gun to kill me. I survived my mother.'

'Thank goodness he didn't injure your sense of humour.'

'That's possibly largely due to the morphine, and unfortunately it's wearing off. I'd like to sit up, but actually it hurts when I move, so I figure I'll just lie here until they bring me some more.'

'Oh, Jamie. I'm so sorry you got hurt.' I take his hand and give it a squeeze.

He turns his head and smiles again, but it's got a slight grimace to it, and it fades completely when his gaze rests on my head. 'You're hurt.'

I touch the bandage on my temple. I guess he was too out of it last night to have noticed. 'I'm okay. He hit me with the gun before he ran off.'

'Bastard! Did they get him?'

'Not yet. The inspector gave me his direct number and I rang first thing this morning. They think he drove up the road, waited until they turned into the driveway, then drove down. He didn't go back to his house. But they're giving me protection until he's caught or they think he's far enough out of state to not be a threat. I'm meeting a couple of constables at home when I'm done here. I think they're hoping he'll come back, so they can catch him.'

'They're using you as bait?'

'Maybe, but I'd rather take a risk and have him out of the game, than live the rest of my life wondering when he might come back.'

Jamie sighs and closes his eyes. A moment later, they flicker open again and he smiles. 'It was a pretty explosive first date, huh?'

'I'm not usually that exciting.'

'I think I'm okay with that, actually.'

I feel an overwhelming urge to kiss this man, but, of course, I don't.

'How about fish and chips on the wharf at Kiama next time?' he asks.

'You want to risk a next time?'

'Is that okay with you?'

I do kiss him. Just lightly, on his forehead.

'Good.' He closes his eyes.

I squeeze his hand again and can't stop grinning.

'I think I'm falling in love,' he murmurs. At least I think that's what he said. It could have been falling asleep, because his mouth opens slightly and his breathing deepens. Looks like visiting hours are over. I refuse to allow myself to think I may have bored him to sleep. I have to get home and finish the editing anyway.

***

The glaziers sent a team up right away, for which I'm grateful because the wind is chilly today. I spent the first part of the morning cleaning up glass, but the activity helped me not to keep remembering that Scott/Dita is still out there and could return.

The house is under the watchful eye of two constables, and despite the fact that the pills aren't killing the headache, I'm working hard on Kelee's story. I've almost finished, and if it goes as smoothly as it has this morning, I'll be able to deliver on time.

But now, I pause and, despite the breeze, sip tea on the veranda. I feel my life is at an impasse, as if the vestiges of my past have been blasted away with those gunshots and my future is completely open. Perhaps it's time for a change. I can't help Jamie's smiling face from floating into my mind.

A Blank Page

This page is intentionally blank.

So That's How it Ends

I click Send, and the manuscript of Kelee's story wings its way across cyber-space to its author. I take a deep breath and push back in my chair. It rolls across the floor and, with a push of my foot, I set it spinning. Round and round I go, grinning like an idiot.

I wonder if Tanya will see the merits of 'my' suggestions and write the story how it really happened. I offered to re-edit the revised parts for free if she did. Stupid of me really, since it's a lot of work, but I would want Kelee to do the same for me if our positions were reversed.

The glaziers have gone and my house smells like putty. Liz is expecting me for dinner—I have to pick up Merlin—and I'll visit Jamie again on the way, but I'm not quite ready to go yet. I want to make sense of the events of the last few days, perhaps of the last few months since Dita began his cyber-stalking.

I decide I'm not going to write reviews anymore.

But snarky me doesn't like that decision—I call her snarky, but she isn't really; she's more the determined and uncompromising part of me.

I tell her it isn't out of fear. I've just lost my taste for it. But it did occur to me that, despite my best intentions, my actions set that chain of events into motion. I didn't deserve the retribution; nothing can absolve Scott from his actions and I'm not responsible for them, but ... you never know how many crazy authors are out there, and I simply can't be bothered dealing with them.

What about the industry? Snarky asks. *About developing a healthy level of critical appraisal?*

I shrug. I suppose I could do what many people do and not post the low star reviews.

Wimp! What about all the readers who deserve to know the quality of the books they're being asked to buy?

I take a deep breath and slip beneath the veil where the fact that there is no universally satisfactory answer to the conundrum simply doesn't matter. I enjoy the stillness and clarity of my mind, and the vibrancy of everything around me. Even the throbbing in my head eases.

Two brain waves emerge from the silence in rapid succession.

I'll not stop writing reviews, good or bad. I'll create a new persona. I'll call her Totally Honest. She'll have no blog, no social media presence, only an account for posting reviews, and no profile—except perhaps for her writing credentials. She'll not deal with authors directly, she'll buy their books. And she'll be untraceable, unrelatable to any physical person. She'll only exist in the cyber-world—the world that transcends national boundaries and doesn't exist anywhere as an actual place.

Snarky is happy. I remind her that she will still have to be polite.

Brainwave two: The recent turn of events in my life makes perfect material for a novel. I shall write it and publish it myself. I doubt it could do worse than *Catnip Creek* did with a mainstream publisher. It will be a thriller, of course. But as I look back over the tapestry of my life, I realise that the strands woven into it come from much further than my corporeal life. My dreams, my cyber-world, my memories, my work, my meditative experience, and those vibrant snippets of life from the yogi in Tibet—whatever they are—are all an integral part of it. Remove one strand and the tapestry would not have the richness of colour and texture of the real thing. Besides, I could not leave out Kelee or the Sage.

I wonder how it will end? My story is not over yet, not for so long as Scott is still out there with a gun, or even out there at all.

Tring tring. Tring tring.

I scoot across the floor to the telephone and lift the handset. 'Hello.'

'Miss Smith.'

'Yes.'

'This is Constable Peters. I'm just ringing to let you know that we have Scott Davidson in custody.'

A weight falls off my shoulders, and tension I'd previously been unaware of fades from my muscles.

'We've charged him with attempted murder, and given the circumstances and his past record, I expect bail will be refused, and he's looking at a guaranteed jail term, so you're safe now, ma'am.'

I'm struck dumb.

'Ma'am. Are you there?'

'Yes, thank you. Thank you very much.'

'The constables will return to the station.'

'Of course.'

'Will you be all right up there by yourself, ma'am?'

'Yes, thank you, I'm fine. Thank you for your concern.'

'No problem, ma'am. We'll be in touch. Have a good day.'

Click.

So that's how it ends.

I wonder if I'll stay true to my word and help Dita with his writing. Will I visit him in prison? I don't want to ever see him again, but ... there's a tug in my heart, an urge to deepen my compassion in a very real way. I push it aside, but the memory of the sobbing little boy stays in my mind. I remind myself that he's also the monster who tried to kill me. I sigh and slot the question into the 'too-hard' basket.

56

Kelee's World

Slade reined in his horse. The dust of the dry plain settled around its hooves as Kelee rode to his side. He looked ahead with a smile, and she followed his gaze. Tall granite towers rose above the trees in the distance—the University of the Warriors.

'Sheldra,' Slade said, nodding his head in satisfaction. Then he turned to her, his eyes twinkling. 'Your father and Beak will never find us here.'

Kelee smiled, but her heart was not as sure as his. She looked back at the foreboding structure. Was she really to become a Warrior? She sighed; what else was there for her now? Her fingers found the clasp engraved with the Menhir family crest at the throat of her purple velvet cloak, and, fumbling in the biting wind, she began to undo it.

Slade frowned. 'What are you doing?'

'We are of the Mage Clans, surely it is best they do not know that.'

Slade chuckled and shook his head, but Kelee saw no humour in the situation. She stared at him stony-faced.

'All Magans are welcome at Sheldra.'

'I would rather not be the subject of their suspicion.' She unclasped the cloak and made to remove it from her shoulders, but he reached out and stayed her hand.

'Keep it on and be proud of who you are, daughter of Lord Menhir,' he said. 'The noble blood of the Magans runs in your veins. Some of your ancestors were the greatest of Warriors.' And yours, Kelee thought. 'When the Warriors here look at you, that is what they will see.'

'Not the daughter of a clan that mocks their beliefs?'

He shook his head. 'Warriors are trained to see the best in people. Besides, only a Magan interested in becoming a Warrior would bother going to Sheldra. Some may even give you extra respect for your boldness as Menhir's daughter.'

Her horse snorted and tossed his head. She drew the reigns tighter. 'My boldness?' She didn't feel bold. The unease in her stomach attested to that.

'In stepping outside the dictates of your position.'

'Ah, yes.' Kelee did not want to be reminded of what she had given up to be with Slade. And it wasn't just the luxury—though the nights spent on hard ground had been softened by Slade's arms around her—she hoped her disappearance would not cause her sick mother to grow weaker.

'Keep it on, love. The wind is still cold.'

Kelee nodded and refastened the clasp, not because he told her to, but because she'd realised that no matter where she went or what she wore, she would always be Lord Menhir's daughter, and that no matter what others thought of him, he was, at heart, a good man. She was proud to be his daughter and of the Menhir line.

Beak and his men, not her father, had chased them through Minion Hills. Her father would forgive her one day, and she could go back, but not until Beak relinquished his claim on her—or until she was married. In the meantime, she would learn the same skills that gave Miramar and Slade their inner peace and strength.

She jabbed her heels into her horse's belly and rode on.

57

The Sage

The Sage sits on the mountain top, his heart wide open from years of meditation. He had always sat there and always would. He no longer knew where his heart stopped and the sky began. His mind blended with space and travelled through all of space and time.

He saw all things and his heart wept. A mother in Gaza sobs hysterically over the dead body of her child, killed by Israeli mortar fire; a child stares numbly at the burnt-out ruins of his home in Australia, hoping his parents escaped the blaze; in India, a husband and wife cling to the roof of a car as floodwaters rush past them; a group of villagers in the Ukraine rush from their homes with a few belongings, wondering where they can go to escape the tanks and guns coming their way. They did not ask for this. They want only to live their lives in peace.

He embraces them all, and every other disaster known to beings, be they large or small—birth, old age, sickness and death, change and the underlying dissatisfaction of those who constantly seek more. He gathers every suffering being into his heart and dissolves their pain in the pulsing formless jewel at its centre.

The earth burns. Its forests and sacred spaces are desecrated, its population too vast for its resources. Hunger increases. Reoccurring floods, giant storms, and earthquakes tear at the fabric of civilisation. Years before, politicians waver or ignore the warnings, thinking only of lining their pockets. Voters vote to safeguard their livelihood only to cast their children's children into starvation. Men fight over land that neither own, and others stone their wives in the street because another man raped her. She is twice cursed. But the sage brings her into his embrace. He brings them all, perpetrator and victim. We are all perpetrators. We are all victims.

He dissolves their suffering into a space vaster than them all, endless in time, existing but never born. The universe clasps its children to its breast, heals their wounds and returns them refreshed and healed to the result of their joint karma. One day they must learn, or be chained forever to the wheel of existence.

A sage sits on a mountain top. He has always sat there and always will. His heart and the sky are the same; his mind one with space and time.

A Note from the Author

Ella's boyfriend Jamie seems to be her perfect match until a death in the family calls him back to England and it becomes clear that he's hiding something. Can their relationship survive the revelation of something so astounding that it completely changes Ella's perception of him and his place in her world? Find out in *The Locksmith's Secret*, out now at all stores.

If you enjoyed this novel, please leave a review at your point of purchase. Not only do I love to know what you think, but also reviews are an important part of helping me to find readers who may enjoy the story. Thank you. I really appreciate your time.

If you'd like to be notified of any new releases or special offers please sign up for my notifications email list. I promise you won't be inundated with emails and you'll be able to unsubscribe at any time. To sign up, visit my website at http://tahlianewland.com and click on the box on the right hand side of the home page.

Follow 'TahliaNewland' on Twitter.
Like 'Tahlia Newland, author,' on Facebook.
Be my fan on Goodreads.

A Special Thank You

A special thank you to Sogyal Rinpoche for providing me with such a comprehensive education in Buddhist philosophy and meditation.

May this book bring benefit to all beings.

Other Great Books

The story of Kelee, which Prunella (Ella) is editing, is an offshoot of the Diamond Peak Series. Readers of that series will be familiar with the world and with the character of her brother Kestril and her mentor Miramar. In this novel, the series is written by a different author.

You can see all my books with links to various purchase points on my website. Though they span genres and ages, all my books are heart-warming and inspiring.

Take a look at:

Happiness Hints: Simple but Profound Slogans to Help You Remember How to be Happy—coming soon.

The award-winning *Diamond Peak Series*—young adult/new adult contemporary fantasy/magical realism. This visionary tale is an analogy for the journey to enlightenment.

A Matter of Perception—a collection of magical realism and urban fantasy short stories on the topic of perception.

A Hole in the Pavement—heart-warming ebook-only magical realism short story from the above collection.

You Can't Shatter Me—an inspiring and empowering young adult magical realism novel on the topic of how to handle a bully. Like Lethal Inheritance, the first book in the Diamond Peak Series, this book has also won two awards, a BRAG Medallion for Outstanding Fiction and the AIA Seal of Excellent in Fiction.

You'll also find a range of quality books in a variety of genres on the Awesome Indies website: http://awesomeindies.net

Tibetan and Australian Glossary

Bardos: the Buddhist term for the transitional states of human experience; in this case the yogi refers to those between death and rebirth.

Blow-up mattress: inflatable mattress.

Buddhadharma: the teachings of the Buddha. Dharma also means the way things are. It's like science in that way.

Chopa: practitioner of the Buddhadarma (teachings of the Buddha).

Dharmapalas practice: a meditation practice with chanting and drums.

Lama: spiritual teacher.

Loo: toilet, bathroom.

Rinpoche: (precious one) a title given to great spiritual teachers and reincarnations of great teachers.

Slanging match: argument. yelling abuse at each other.

Tangkhas: paintings of deities and mandalas.

Tonglen: a meditation practice for arousing compassion.

Tsampa: ground and roasted barley. The Tibetans mix it with water or yak milk —the Tibetan take-away.

Vajra: Tibetan sceptre. Represents the nature of reality.

About the Author

Multi-award-winning author Tahlia Newland writes heart-warming and inspiring fantasy and literary fiction. She has published seven novels, one book of short stories and a couple of non-fiction books on writing and happiness.

Tahlia is an editor for AIA Publishing, a selective author-funded publishing company. She also makes masks and steampunk accessories and is an online meditation coach dedicated to bringing the wisdom of meditation to people the world over. Visit her blog for great articles on various aspects of meditation.

Before turning to full time writing and editing, she had over twenty years' experience in scripting and performing in Visual Theatre and Theatre in Education. She is also a trained teacher who taught high school creative and performing arts for several years.

Tahlia has had extensive training in Buddhist meditation and philosophy. She lives in Australia with a husband and a couple of cheeky Burmese cats, and she wears steampunk clothing because beautiful clothes deserve to be worn.